Side by Side in Life and Death

Michelle came, waiting impatiently while I unhooked her leash with the words, "Go find him now."

And as I spoke those words, a sense of foreboding swept over me so strong that I shivered. After the search, I reflected on that rush of coldness: I wasn't psychic. Michelle had signaled me with something barely perceptible in her manner, but a change that I could intuit. That shows you how closely an SAR trainer and his dog are tuned. Michelle and I have not come upon death often, but when it is out there, we both know it.

Michelle and Me

*The Incredible True Stories
of a K-9 Search-and-Rescue Team*

Tom Shelby with **Victoria Houston**

BERKLEY BOOKS, NEW YORK

Although these events actually took place, certain names, places, and identifying characteristics have been altered to protect the privacy of individuals.

MICHELLE AND ME

A Berkley Book / published by arrangement with
Koerner Kronenfeld Partners, LLC

PRINTING HISTORY
Berkley edition / February 2002

All rights reserved.
Copyright © 2002 by Koerner Kronenfeld Partners, LLC
Book design by Julie Rogers
Cover design by Steven Ferlauto
Cover photograph by Jaye Shelby
This book, or parts thereof, may not be reproduced in
any form without permission.
For information address: The Berkley Publishing Group,
a division of Penguin Putnam Inc.,
375 Hudson Street, New York, New York 10014.

Visit our website at
www.penguinputnam.com

ISBN: 0-425-18451-X

BERKLEY®
Berkley Books are published by The Berkley Publishing Group,
a division of Penguin Putnam Inc., 375 Hudson Street,
New York, New York 10014.
BERKLEY and the "B" design
are trademarks belonging to Penguin Putnam Inc.

PRINTED IN THE UNITED STATES OF AMERICA

10 9 8 7 6 5 4 3 2 1

Thanks to Ivan Kronenfeld for the idea to write this book, to Victoria Houston, and to Susan Allison and Berkley Publishing.

Tara, Kerry and Brett—thanks for being great kids.

Special thanks to Jaye, wife, closest friend and strongest critic, who said things to me that nobody else had the nerve to say.

To Frank Lumia, a great unpaid editor and search partner. There are acquaintances, friends, best friends and brothers—thank you for being there, brother.

And, of course, to Michelle—who has added so much inspiration to my life by sharing her canine spirit with me.

Contents

Foreword
A Portrait of the Author and His Dog

*A sturdy, broad-shouldered man with perceptive, un-*derstanding eyes, Tom Shelby is not just another nationally prominent dog trainer.

Nor is his partner, Michelle, just another search-and-rescue dog.

Together, as a canine search-and-rescue team, they are unique in their abilities and their experiences, which Shelby chronicles in this book.

But if as a team they save lives, as a professional dog trainer, Shelby also saves carpets, family, sanity and much more, of course.

"It's amazing how much of my life revolves around feces and urine," he said recently in his self-deprecating way.

He is too modest. Shelby's canine clients answer to such masters as actor Eddie Murphy, authors David Halberstam and Erica Jong, actress Linda Dano, and many more Manhattan residents of national and international renown.

This is in addition to his work in K-9 SAR (canine search and rescue) as a unit leader and a trainer. *Accident* is a word that recurs in a look at these parallel tracks in Shelby's career:

- he stumbled into his career by *accident*
- he trains dogs (and owners) to minimize *accidents* and other behavioral problems
- and, all kidding aside, his search-and-rescue work with Michelle is dedicated to rescuing people caught up in the life-threatening *accident* known as "being lost"

Tom Shelby never planned to be a professional dog trainer—ever. "With the exception of apprenticing to Seeing Eye dog trainers, I don't think a formal school for trainers like me even existed when I got into this field in 1972," he said.

A veteran of four and a half years of teaching junior high and high school students, he had taken a brief respite from academia to share the ownership and the onus of running a small moving company with friends—until, that is, he and his buddies collided with the bureaucracy of New York's Department of Transportation.

While exploring these two dissimilar career options, Shelby was also learning how to coexist with nature as he shared two consecutive apartments with roommates that included humans, hamsters, fish, birds, snakes, cats and dogs. Litters of the latter.

"My life was a menagerie," said Shelby, thinking

back, "but the apartments were clean and they didn't smell, even if my friends and I called our apartments Animal House I and Animal House II. I didn't realize it at the time, but my apartment living was like going to an animal behavior graduate school. I was able to observe the interactions of the cats and dogs while learning that the ideal way to be educated is through entertainment. You cannot learn any better than when you are totally entertained by your subject matter."

Curiously enough, his studies in animal behavior led to romance. One of the ties that bound him to wife-to-be Jaye was his hugely successful, albeit amateur, training of her dog Noelle. Jaye had left Noelle in Shelby's company while traveling abroad. "By the end of the two weeks, I had trained Noelle to do a handful of tricks, which she performed beautifully," said Shelby. He was being trained, too—"Not only did I find it easy to train Noelle, but it was great fun and very rewarding."

Not so the moving business. At the same time that Shelby and his friends disbanded their small company, he and Jaye made plans to decide on their next career moves—after taking a long vacation. They stopped by his parents' home to discuss the pros and cons of Alaska versus South America, but before the travelogue got under way, Shelby took a few minutes to read the newspaper. By accident, he found himself cruising the Help Wanted section.

"This ad jumped out at me: *Dog Trainer Wanted. Experience Necessary,*" recalls Shelby. "I remember it like it was this morning. Within fifteen seconds of reading that ad, I was on the phone with the owner of the American Dog Training Academy. When I got off the phone, Jaye and my mom were staring at me very strangely.

" 'Am I in the twilight zone or did you just pass your-self off as a veteran dog trainer for a job interview to-morrow?' asked Jaye."

"The absurdity of it all made me burst out laughing, then they laughed, too, and soon we were all roaring with hilarity. That was Tuesday. I hadn't even been looking for a job, not even thinking about it. I got hired on Wednesday to start work the following Monday. Needless to say, we never made our trip."

Instead, he was given a list of thirty-five people with whom to set up appointments in order to continue their lessons. "I did that," said Shelby, "I also, before Monday, read *Good Dog, Bad Dog* by Mathew Margolis and *The Koehler Method of Guard Dog Training* by William Koehler." He appeared for work on Monday and hasn't looked back. Today Tom Shelby is one of Manhattan's best-known dog trainers, with over one thousand training appointments annually.

In the years immediately following his entry into the field, Shelby had the opportunity to learn from the best. "I worked in attack training under Ed Rivera. That was a terrific learning experience, working with really tough dogs. What I learned there about canine aggression has served me well over the years. I also worked for Mathew Margolis and became one of his two top trainers until he moved to California." Later he worked with Brian Kilcommons of the Professional School of Dog Training and author of the best-selling *Good Owners, Great Dogs*. He has also run the group training lessons for Manhattan's Bide-A-Wee and the Humane Society.

*   *   *

Along the way, Michelle changed his life. Feminine and powerful with muscle rippling beneath her sleek, soft fur, Michelle is a thirteen-year-old Doberman pinscher who has led her master on search-and-rescue missions that would challenge the average K-9 SAR unit. This partnership with Michelle as a K-9 SAR team has been a focus of Shelby's personal life for over a decade.

In 1986 he began his official K-9 SAR training and in 1988 helped found Amigo Canine Search and Rescue. Marion Hardy, one of the nation's pioneers in SAR, certified him in 1990 as a member of the Hug-a-Tree Program, which is dedicated to finding lost children. Shelby is also active as a special deputy sheriff in the Rockland County Sheriff's Department K-9 Search and Rescue Unit—for whom he and Michelle participate in searches and in demonstrations for the public on SAR techniques.

Unlike the discovery of his vocation, his teaming up with Michelle was no accident.

"Michelle joined our family when she was twelve weeks old," said Shelby. "I had gotten a call from the breeder and went out to look at the pups. At first, I wasn't sure. The mother was a little too protective and territorial for my family situation."

Michelle, who was one of four pups available from the litter, took matters into her own hands, recalls Shelby. "She got my attention immediately by walking up to me out of curiosity, looking me in the eye and saying, 'Hi, let's play!'

"Thirteen years later, she still plays at the drop of a hat. She passed all my tests that day, so we took her home. Jaye drove while I held her in my lap, and I remember saying to Jaye, 'I have no feeling for a name.'

Jaye said, 'She's Michelle.' The pup lifted her head and looked at Jaye and that was that."

Shelby has since been surprised by the reactions of some to his owning a Doberman. "Because I am a professional trainer and because Michelle is a search-and-rescue dog, I am often asked what breed of dog I own. I'll answer, 'A Dobe,' and watch their jaws drop in dismay. Too many people underestimate Dobermans. The exception is other Dobe owners who know how wonderful this breed can be.

"When I am asked by someone who *really* wants to know why Michelle and I are a team, I am happy to tell them, because to simply say that Michelle is a 'working dog'—the classic definition of a purebred Doberman pinscher—is to sell her short. Instead, here is what I say: If the American Kennel Club defines seven groups of purebreds, each with a winning characteristic, then my dog possesses the best of each—all wrapped up in one.

"She has the powerful body of the Doberman breed but her eyes are those of a spaniel: pools of soft understanding. She can be as comic as a pug, as agile as a sporting dog, as tuned to the wind as a scent hound and as bullheaded and persevering as a terrier. She is also feline. A thirteen-year member of our close-knit family, she purrs like a cat when hugged by any one of us—mom, dad or kids.

"When it comes to search-and-rescue ability, she is exceptional. Here is where her breed makes a difference," emphasized Shelby. "People have approximately five million olfactory cells in their noses but a Doberman has over one hundred million. A dog like Michelle actually smells the millions and millions of scent particles of skin that are constantly dropping off our bodies. She smells these in the air. We call that 'air scenting.' This is different from a bloodhound who tracks the footsteps of a person who passed through an area hours earlier, because that dog is smelling the minute scent particles left *on the ground*.

"When an air-scenting dog, like Michelle, raises its nose to the wind, you cannot hide certain signposts that would escape another dog or type of rescuer."

Signposts that lead to rescues from life-and-death situations. Rescues, searches and related experiences that Tom Shelby recounts in riveting detail in the pages that follow, along with training tips from his years of experience.

—VICTORIA HOUSTON

1

A Haunting Search, One of Our First

This was a search that haunted me for a long, long time. At first, I would remember and shudder. Now I just wince in pain. Funny thing about these searches: sometimes you do everything right but the result is tragedy; other times blunder follows blunder and the result is great.

It was autumn. Jaye, our three kids and I were spending a few days at our cottage in the country, enjoying the feel and smell of the brisk November air. Even though we live outside the city in what some people think is the country, our cottage is different. Our friends teased us when we first bought it, "What do you need a country house for? You already live in the country!"

I would then try to explain the difference between countrified suburbia and real country, but I gave up. For us, the reality was that buying our cottage was one of the smartest things we ever did. Here is where we re-charge our batteries, tighten our family bonds and just plain enjoy nature. Not only do we ice skate on our pond in winter, swim in it in the summer—but it is ideal for K-9 search-and-rescue training.

And that is how it happened that my good friend Ed Rivera also moved here. A fellow dog trainer, Ed and his family spent several weekends with us and fell in love with the country. Once they moved here, Ed and I spent a great deal of time working our dogs on mock searches.

This was great for me because when it came to "read-ing" tough dogs, Ed was one of the best. Rumor had it that he could climb a junkyard fence, take the collar off the resident guard dog and hang it on the office door with his business card. Actually, that's not just a ru-mor—I know it's true. I saw it happen years ago at a gas station in Brooklyn.

Unlike me, Ed didn't move to the country just for the weekends, he moved here permanently after landing a job as a counselor at a local correctional institute for boys ages sixteen and under. This turned out to be per-fect: a great job for him and ideal for our joint dog training purposes.

The advantages were many: our houses were just twelve miles apart, we were located deep in the Catskill Mountains with excellent territory for search training, and the facility where Ed counseled inmates was nearby. The latter worked for our training purposes as we had permission from the authorities to involve several of the boys in our training efforts—we would send them into the woods to hide and use the dogs to find them. Fun for the boys, excellent working opportunity for the dogs.

As it happened, not long after we launched these exercises, there was an attempted escape from the correctional facility. Calls went out to the counselors and Ed and Abu, his German shepherd, were immediately enlisted in the search for the runaways. To everyone's astonishment, Abu found the boys within an hour!

The story of how that happened still puts a smile on our faces. Apparently Ed and Abu came upon the three escapees in a small clearing where they had sat down to rest. It was nothing dramatic—man and dog just stepped into the circle and Ed said a calm "Hello." But the boys froze at the sight of the dog. They were speechless. Finally, one mustered the nerve to protest, "We ain't goin' back."

This posed a slight conundrum for Ed, who, more interested in the thrill of the hunt and the test of Abu's skills, had not given much thought to what he would do if they actually apprehended the boys. He wasn't armed and a search-and-rescue dog is trained to find people, not eat them. But Ed could see the boys didn't know that.

So he looked at the culprits and said, "You may not be going back, but you also are not leaving!" Whereupon he turned to Abu and said, "Down—Stay—and Watch." The "Watch" command meant nothing to Abu, but being a dominant curious German shepherd, she immediately lay down and stared intently at the boys. Her ears, face and body registered every movement the boys made. Intimidated by her intense concentration, the boys stayed very, very still. Ed, meanwhile, shot off a flare to signal the find and the cavalry arrived shortly thereafter. Thus was Ed and Abu's fabulous reputation established.

Within two years of this episode, Ed and I and Frank
Lumia founded our Amigo K-9 Search and Rescue Unit.
A few words about Frank, who is an unusual guy. We
met when he sold us our house but, in addition to selling
real estate, he is an award-winning karate instructor,
sings for fun, is an expert magician and has become one
of my closest friends. And so it was that with the addition of Frank, our K-9 unit was now composed of three
guys and their dogs—Abu, Ed's German shepherd;
Michelle, my Doberman pinscher; and Yogi, Frank's
Bernese mountain dog.

At the time the six of us were getting together, Michelle was just over one year old and Abu, at two, was
about eight months older. Abu is also the only dog ever
to dominate Michelle. Though they were the best of
friends since puppyhood—and would play fight for
hours, Abu never let Michelle forget who was the boss.
The only time I ever saw Michelle stand up to Abu was
during a search.

Michelle was working, searching for an article
dropped by a man—what we call an "article find." This
was a training exercise and Michelle was sitting in the
middle of a field by a glove that had been dropped. Sitting is how she is supposed to indicate an article has
been found. This is preferred over retrieving the article
because there may be more clues at the article site. If
it's a crime scene then nothing should be disturbed. Although she was sitting now, over the years she brought
me the articles and for some reason I lacked the resolve
to correct this behavior. I feared the negativity she might
feel.

So that day Michelle was sitting at her article find
when suddenly Abu bounded out of nowhere and ran up

to grab the glove. Michelle, refusing to let that happen, chased Abu from the site. This was a level of aggression from Michelle that was new to me, but reassuring. It meant that this Doberman pup took her work seriously. Abu got the message and backed off. She knew she was wrong to interfere with Michelle when she was working; Michelle demanded territorial respect and Abu deferred, as she should have.

Once Abu dropped the challenge, Michelle dropped the aggressive action. She was happy again. That reminds me of why I do this work. The given is that working dogs are happiest when they're working just as scent hounds are happiest when they're tracking and retrievers when they're retrieving. The same goes for us SAR humans, too—we're happiest when our dogs are happy.

Another aspect of our new Amigo K-9 SAR Unit was that we were very likely to be the first responders to a scene, mainly because we were unique. There were no other K-9 units nearby. This meant the scene would be relatively uncontaminated by other searchers and that, in turn, made finds easier. Also, if we found anyone, it was likely to be the person for whom we were searching as this was a remote, if not desolate, region.

But even as I say that, I need to point out that over the years Michelle has found plenty of people we *weren't* looking for—hikers, lovers, campers, etc. One of the funnier situations was when she "found" a young couple who thought they were safe smooching away in the depths of the forest, only to have Michelle come leaping through the brush and barking so happily at her find that she scared the bejesus out of the couple. Another time she came on a man and a woman having a picnic, their lunch laid out on a blanket in a clearing.

Michelle trotted right up to the man, leaped into his lap and licked his face with great enthusiasm, as if to say, "Thank God I found you and you're okay."

I came on the scene, saw his face rigid with terror as she licked away, and I knew the poor guy thought he was going to die. He told me later, when his heart had resumed a normal beat, "When that Doberman jumped into my lap, I thought this is it, this is the end."

One of our best "finding the un-lost stories" is when Michelle found a woman picking flowers who, when asked if she was lost, insisted, "No." But when we asked her where she came from and where she was going, she had no idea. Nor did she have an explanation, it turned out later, for being eight hours late returning to her point of origin. Still, she insisted she wasn't lost. Thank you, Michelle, for your persistence in finding.

But back to that crisp November day in the Catskills that I started to tell you about a few pages ago. Evening was settling in and my family and I were hanging out at Frank's with his wife, Debbie. The night promised to be perfect for sitting by the fire as it hissed and popped. Down in Frank's music studio, our kids were happily singing and recording themselves while upstairs us adults, full from a tasty meal, sat by the hearth with cognac in hand. We considered the pros and cons of bundling up for a trip to the deck to smoke a cigar.

As if she could read our minds, Michelle gave a loud groan of comfort and contentment and sank even deeper into the lush carpet—she wasn't going to sit on a hard, frozen deck just to smell cigar smoke! Frank and I caught her expression and laughed. We decided we weren't going anywhere after all. We were much too comfortable—warm, full and tired. It had been a vigorous day and, as Michelle had just reminded us, it was time to kick back.

We were close to dozing off when the phone rang. It was Sheriff Adams: *"Missing Person."* Frank held the phone to his chest as he repeated the sheriff's words. *MISSING PERSON*. My heart did a hop, skip and a jump. When your partner is a search dog, those are the two most powerful words you can hear. They certainly propelled me up out of my comfortable chair and into action.

Frank was still on the phone getting the details—". . . it's an elderly man with Parkinson's Disease lost in the woods . . . the police told me you have a dog that can find lost people and you're happy to help at any time. . . ."

I was listening with the usual questions running through my head: "Help at any time. . . ." Did I really say that? Did I really say that at any time I would stop whatever I was doing and take on the responsibility of going into the forest to hunt for a missing person? What if Michelle and I can't find the person and they die? What if it's a child lost? What if it's pouring rain or sleeting? Or I have a major headache or the flu? That happened once. I got a call for a teenage boy missing in a blizzard and I was coming down with something—but the boy was the same age as my daughter, so I went.

Frank's expression as he held the phone to his ear changed. He looked stunned. But then SAR work was quite new to him still, and so I took the phone and asked a number of critical questions. Then I gave the phone back to Frank so he could get directions to the search site.

Finally, he hung up and looked at me. Reality was

dawning. "Jesus, Tom," he said, "this is Amigo's first legit search!" True enough. Up until now, our only searches were for the boys gone AWOL from Ed's correctional facility, and Ed had handled most of those on the spot. This was our first call from an outside agency, and the sheriff, no less!

If Frank was a little shaky at the idea of our first Amigo search, I was still reeling from the impact of the words *missing person*. I liken the feeling to a jolting gear change. It's as if you go from reverse to forward bypassing neutral, from a state of total relaxation to one of intense energy and all in the few seconds that it takes for those two words to sink in. I describe it as a state of intense energy driven by a complex mix of feelings: the seriousness of the life-or-death situation, the fear of failure, and an awareness of the extreme physical and mental exertions I'm about to undertake. But that's the anxiety side of search-and-rescue work. It is also unbelievably exciting, exhilarating and—dare I say it—fun. *But deadly serious fun.*

As Frank hung up the phone, we moved into a frantic rush mode for several seconds, both of us accomplishing absolutely nothing. I still held my glass of cognac, most of which had spilled over my wrist and hand. I remember telling myself I needed to wash it off so the sheriff wouldn't smell it and think some drunken hombre with a dog was showing up.

"What are we taking?" Frank asked. I could hear the nervous tension in his voice.

Jaye intervened, sensible as always. "We'll put some energy snacks together for you. I'll stay here with Debbie until you return. Do you need water for the dogs?"

"No," I said, settling down and getting a grip on things, "there's plenty out there."

Before packing our vests, I reviewed the situation weather-wise. We knew the victim was elderly, ill with Parkinson's, and had been missing since the afternoon, when he went for a walk and presumably got lost during a snow squall. We knew the snow squall because we'd been in it, too. And it had been something.

The brief storm had not covered the entire county, just pockets—but where it passed, it wreaked havoc. Lasting about half an hour, the squall had caught Frank and me by surprise. Out enjoying the fall day, we were on my ATV crossing an open field about 2,000 feet from the summit of a nearby mountain when suddenly the wind picked up.

Within thirty seconds, we were blinded by wind-driven snow. In fact, the first blast was so forceful and unexpected that we laughed in surprise. Then the combination of a sudden wind chill and wet snow left us numb with cold. The laughing stopped, the ATV stopped and the fun stopped. I had a space blanket under the seat so we hurried to tie the grommet strings to the handle-bars and rear fender. Sitting with our backs to the side of the ATV, we pulled the blanket over our heads and held it to the ground with our feet and hands. We had Michelle and Yogi in there, too, keeping us warm and cozy. Now it was fun again—and the rest of the storm lasted no longer than twenty minutes.

Thinking back over that episode, I remembered Frank saying as we held the blanket in place and listened to the wind howl and the snow pound that he would hate to be stuck out in a storm like this. Then we laughed because that is exactly what was happening—we were stuck. But we were so warm and comfy, we didn't want it to end. Nor did Yogi, who has a coat like a St. Bernard, or Michelle, who was snuggled between Frank and me. We were all a little disappointed when the squall cleared.

But thinking back over that brief episode helped me be sure we were fully prepared by the time we got on our way, which was ten minutes after the sheriff's call had come in. Critical to our efforts would be our Amigo K-9 SAR uniforms: utility-orange survey vests with ample pockets to carry all our stuff. Our stuff consists of flares, orange plastic marking tape, glow necklaces, energy snacks for people and dogs, water, flashlights, first aid kits and anything else that might be needed, depending on the situation and territory.

The equipping and packing of these vests had been an important part of our Amigo training and we had spent a great deal of time discussing, arguing over and revising the list of contents. Each vest was packed slightly differently according to which individual would wear it because each of us had different needs and perceptions, not to mention skills. You ask yourself questions like— Do I take rope? If so, how much can I carry? For me, for example, glow necklaces, which we get at weddings and bar mitzvahs, are mandatory for my vest. I put them around Michelle's neck so I can see her in the dark. When she is working off-leash, often quite far from me, the iridescent purple or green rings may appear surreal but they keep me informed of where my "nuclear dog" is.

That's what I call her in the dark—nuclear dog. By now, I am so familiar with that eerie sight—ghostly rings of neon color floating through black forest—that I am able to tell from changes in the movement of the rings if and when Michelle has found a human scent.

As Frank drove, I unpacked two glow necklaces. Meanwhile, in the backseat Michelle was pumped, pacing the seat and whining. I was pumped myself and her mood reflected mine. Dogs are often extremely aware of people's moods and Michelle has an uncanny ability to read mine.

At home, her leash is hung where she can reach it. When I'm planning to take her somewhere I tell her to bring me her leash and Tri's, (my other dog), too, if he is to come along. For some reason, she always insists on making two trips. She knows what I want, but she refuses to bring both at once. I'm not sure why.

I'll never forget one example of her ESP. It was a day that she and I were home alone and I decided to take a walk. But I didn't say a word. Instead, I left Michelle sleeping on the sunroom floor while I went upstairs to get a jacket. When I came down a few minutes later, Michelle was sitting in the middle of the room with the leash in her mouth. (And only one leash, not Tri's.) Now how did she know what was on my mind? She is so sensitive.

Another example happened when my son was a toddler, running a high fever, and fell asleep with half his body on top of Michelle. For three hours, that wonderful Doberman did not move for fear of waking the little guy. She herself was awake most of that time, which showed me the incredible restraint she exercised.

Right now, as Frank continued to drive toward the command post, which was thirty minutes from his house, Michelle's mild fidgeting in the backseat reminded me to settle down and formulate a plan of action. Especially because this was Amigo's first "call-out," we wanted to make a professional presentation. Frank, having never been on a search, was looking to me for direction.

"What do we do first when we get there?" he asked.

At this point, I was thinking that even if it was his first search, I couldn't imagine many people I'd rather have at my side than Frank.

"You're my 'co-op,' " I said. "I'll handle Michelle, I need to keep my eyes on her. You work the radio and keep us from getting lost. Once we arrive, we'll talk to the sheriff, get a profile on the victim, see if there's anything else the sheriff knows, see if there is a PLS (place last seen), hope for a clean scent article—"

Frank cut me off: "How do we start Michelle?"

That's what I love about Frank—he cuts to the chase faster than anyone. "I dunno yet. It'll depend on a lot of things, I'll figure it out when it's time."

Just then Michelle put her head on my shoulder. She was standing on the backseat and leaning forward to nuzzle the side of her face against mine. I loved it. Besides the warm, soft feel of her, I knew what she was telling me—and I loved her all the more for it. She was glowing with controlled excitement, anticipation of the fun of the hunt—the smells, the new woods, the sounds, the incredible thrill of the "find." Best of all, she wasn't jumping around, yapping to get started. Instead, she was acknowledging our partnership, acknowledging my role in our upcoming adventure. She was focusing her intense anticipation into controlled energy, which she made me feel through the side of her face. *She was sharing her excitement with me!*

I find this to be an incredible feeling—like a Vulcan mind meld. And so, holding my face against Michelle's,

I said to Frank, "Michelle will tell me where to start."

A minute later, Frank said, "When we get there, who will be in charge?" Another good question and one that popped me right into gear. *I would be in charge.* My heart raced as I told him, "We'll be running the show. Technically the sheriff is in charge but we'll be calling all the shots."

"We're almost there," said Frank. At the sound of his voice, Michelle lifted her head off my shoulder and whined softly. At that moment, I felt totally tuned into Michelle, totally sensitive to her language, and, boy, was she "humming" language at that point. This is true teamwork: she complements me with her one hundred million olfactory cells, her terrific speed and agility, her intelligence, her extreme enjoyment of the controlled freedom, and best of all, her powerful need to please me. There is nothing like the single-minded purpose of a working dog, totally focused on the search with no thoughts of mortgage payments or orthodontist bills. I give direction, she has the skills.

Suddenly we could see flashing lights up ahead. Lots of flashing lights. At least it seemed that way, perhaps because we were in a valley between some mountains in the middle of nowhere. Sheriff Adams introduced himself as I got out of the car. Nearby was the emergency rescue vehicle, a school bus painted red.

Adams told us that Mr. Baker was in his late sixties and that even though he had Parkinson's, he was able to enjoy "reasonably long walks." I asked how long is "reasonably long"? He didn't answer. Instead, he said, "How do you want to proceed?"

Then I asked a lot of questions. The sheriff had done a good job gathering information so we had a good description of our victim, an idea of what his state of mind was, what he was wearing, and, best of all, a PLS. I asked where Baker's house was and Adams pointed over my shoulder in the direction we had come from.

"What are we doing here?" I asked.

"He was last seen near here, by the house up the hill and around the bend," said Adams. Given that, I told Adams that I'd probably start the dog near the house. I asked if he had the clean scent article I had requested. He pointed to the police car across the street.

"Do you think it's *really* clean?" I had been very clear in our earlier phone conversation on exactly what constitutes "clean" when it comes to scent articles. Baker's wife had assured Adams that no one else had touched her husband's pillow. Adams took the pillow off the bed himself, using a pair of pliers and making sure not to touch it, then he had placed it in a new plastic bag, which in turn was placed on a newspaper that Baker had been reading earlier. The newspaper was also in the backseat of the police car, also placed there by Adams with pliers.

"Great," I said, "let's go talk to the person who saw Baker last. But before we go to the house, please have all cars and trucks moved about two hundred yards downwind and the engines turned off. Gasoline fumes will immediately and temporarily destroy a dog's smelling ability."

That done, we drove about a quarter mile to the house around the bend to speak with the lady who saw our victim last. We stood in her living room looking out through the bay window as she pointed to the exact spot where she was sure he had actually walked. It was time for Michelle!

As the lady chatted on about why she just happened to be by the window as Baker passed, I saw Michelle across the lawn standing on the car seat and staring out of Frank's car window. And I loved what I saw—an intense, calm, peaceful, patient look. She knew the best was about to come and was relishing the wait in a state of relaxed readiness. It was beautiful. Her eyes were shining, reflecting the beams from headlights. Her body was so shiny it looked metallic. To me, she looked like "Robot Dog," the Arnold Schwarzenegger of Dogland.

I tore my eyes away from Robot Dog to thank the lady for her valuable help. Then I headed for Michelle. On the way to Frank's car, Adams asked, "What happens now?"

"Hopefully I can find a real 'scent pool' and leave the rest to Michelle," I said. When I got to the car, I opened the door and stepped back as I softly said, "OK." That was Michelle's cue to exit the car.

We crossed back to the PLS, where she raced around the lady's lawn to release pent-up energy. She always does that. As a young pup, she was useless for the first few minutes of a search. But in early training sessions we developed a pattern whereby I stand around and laughingly curse at her for about ten minutes until she gets the nervous energy out of her system. One time, during a mock search, I had unwittingly entertained a whole group of people at a distant base camp when I left my radio on and they could hear ten minutes of my calling my dog everything imaginable. And so she ran and I joshed until we were both ready.

Now I went over to Sheriff Adams's car and got the pillow in the plastic bag while telling Frank to suit up for an extended walk in the woods. We put on our vests, double-checked our equipment (extra batteries are a must), and I told Frank I would now expose Michelle to the scent article at a point where I thought a Baker scent pool might be.

A scent pool is created when a person stops in one place for a few moments for whatever reason. Millions of microscopic skin particles are constantly falling off of our bodies twenty-four hours a day, thus, whenever we pause, we leave a pool of scent particles behind. Invisible to us, to a dog like Michelle it is a veritable Olympic-sized pool of scent.

Our witness had said she saw Baker stop to tie his shoe and she had pointed to the exact spot where he had stopped. This was where I intended to scent Michelle on the pillow. I hoped that she could immediately locate the scent pool from there and set off on Baker's trail. While this would be actual tracking, my intent was not to remain on the actual path taken by Baker but to follow him as the crow flies. This would cut off hours of walking, which was critical if we were to reach our elderly, infirm victim before he got dangerously cold.

As Frank and I were adjusting the flashlights we wore on our heads, I explained my strategy to Adams that I hoped Michelle could make a beeline for Baker. What I did not tell Adams was that that is not always as great as it sounds. If the person we're searching for walks along a straight path or road for a mile, then makes a ninety-degree left turn for another mile, we might be better off following the actual path than cutting left through the woods. Besides the possibility of getting lost ourselves, the woods can be dangerous or difficult to get through.

But on the other hand, a lost person can be traveling

fast in huge circles so following their route can take hours or days, whereas an air-scenting dog might turn around and walk you right into their path as they're headed your way. But I didn't want to get into all that with the good sheriff at this moment. Whatever the options and the risks, the axiom is *Trust the dog!* That was the only point I wanted to make.

It was time. Frank and I were geared up and Michelle had taken the edge off her extra energy and relieved herself (at the edge of the woods, thankfully). I walked her over to the best spot. I was prepared to psyche her up before I pointed to the ground, then tell her to "Go find!" But all I actually got to say was "Go fi—"

With one quick sniff, she was off and down the road in the very direction the lady had pointed. What made me think she still needed so much direction? She scented so quickly and moved out so fast, I felt a little foolish. She knows her work and is not into drum roll starts any longer. When she was a pup in training she loved the big psyche-up starts, but now it's more "let the games begin."

After the initial shock of "Holy shit, she's got it, she's on his trail," Frank and I were trotting along after Michelle, who was way ahead of us. There is nothing like seeing your dog sailing down the road nose to the ground. It's the greatest feeling, better than the salesman hearing "yes," better than a coon hunter hearing his hounds baying, better than the fisherman seeing his bobber pulled underwater. It's not as good as sex, but very close.

The distance between Michelle and us was increasing at an alarming rate. The last thing I wanted was to exhaust Frank and myself in the first fifteen minutes of a search by running after the dog. Plus, she was clearly on the actual footpath, she wasn't air scenting at all. I didn't want her to miss a turnoff by overrunning it in her enthusiasm, so I yelled, "Wait." I had to repeat it twice before she slowed enough for us to catch up. For about fifteen minutes she stayed to one side of the road, moving slower than she wanted to, but I insisted. Normally, I would have put a line on her because of the nearness of the road, but I hadn't seen a car since we started, so I didn't.

Suddenly she stopped abruptly and sniffed around, then just as abruptly dashed across the road and into thick brush and undergrowth. I heard barking. Heart pounding, I pushed through the brush to a wooden fence. Behind it was a field with horses. I couldn't see how many but they were startled and skittish, which is what had caused Michelle to bark.

Did Baker cut across this field? I called Michelle back to my side of the fence to restart her and see what we had. He may have crossed just to look at the horses and then continued, or Michelle may just have decided to take a horse-seeing break.

As it was, Michelle came back through the fence, yelped once as though hurt or startled, and that was it. I thought no more about the diversion and directed her back to a point just beyond where she had crossed the road. I told her to settle down and continue searching. She sniffed about for a few seconds, then continued down the road as before, obviously still on the scent.

"What was that about?" asked Frank.

"Beats me." Ten minutes later, still heading down the side of the road in pitch-blackness, I could see a change in the pace and movement of the glow necklace. Michelle was meandering, she must have missed a turnoff. I called her back to where I was sure she had still been on-scent and told her to settle down and work it out.

This is the hardest part of a search—helping the dog refind a scent that has been lost. You help by not helping, which takes conscious effort and self-control. This is where I'm trained and conditioned and the dog is not!

I once spent a weekend in a cabin deep in the Poconos with a seventy-something veteran bloodhound handler who taught by repetition. I must have heard him say, "Can't do shit," five trillion times in three nights and two days. If you're training the dog and you know where the trail is and you lead, hint or direct the dog in any way to that trail, then your dog will be less trustworthy. Instead, you tell yourself, "I can't do shit, let the dog do it." *What I learned from that bloodhound old-timer I try never to forget: Tell yourself, "I can't do shit," and let your dog work it out.*

As Frank and I waited quietly, "not doing shit," the night grew a little less dark. While keeping an eye on the glow necklace, we took the time to look around us. The clouds had disappeared and the sky was bright with stars. A slight breeze had come up, turning the night air colder. But it was nice out there in the dark, the sky was beautiful.

I was enjoying the break when Frank asked a question that took the peace out of the quiet: "What if we find this guy and he's in bad shape, hypothermic? What do we do with him?"

"Get him as warm as possible as fast as we can and get him transported out," I said. "What we have to do is find him as soon as possible. Since we have no idea what we're going to find, we'll deal with that then. Right now, let's just find him." At this point, I was feeling pretty confident, I just had a feeling we couldn't miss. There were no other dogs looking for him, none even close by. If we could just refind that scent, this would be our first Amigo find.

But over the next twenty minutes, as Michelle me-andered, my confidence wavered. Then it happened. It wasn't obvious at first—but it seemed like the glow necklace got stuck in one position about a foot off the ground. It was pretty weird watching this ghostly blue-green ring of light frozen in space.

Afraid she was sniffing deer droppings or animal scat, I turned my flashlight on Michelle's glow necklace. I try to keep the light off as much as possible in order to keep my night vision sharp and to save the batteries, but I needed to check. No droppings. My heart did a little two-step as I kept the flashlight on her. She sniffed a small area pretty intensely, then did one of her pig snorts, a disgusting slurping sound she makes when she gets a good whiff of something she's looking for, and headed left off the road into a field at a zigzag with her head down.

I got excited.

"Am I reading this right?" asked Frank as we fol-lowed her into the field.

"We're going to find this guy!"

We were on a path perpendicular to the road and crossing a series of huge fields toward the woods. The fields had patches of snow, which made it easier to see even as clouds were rolling back in, causing the night to get darker and colder again. I yelled to Michelle to wait once and to go easy twice in order to slow her down a little. I didn't want her to lose the trail again.

Then Michelle veered right, parallel to the woods. Again it was a weird sight. We would see Michelle as she crossed a patch of snow, then all we could see would be the floating glow necklace skimming across the fields. Sometimes the necklace would stop, jerk around, then take off again. I remember thinking that someone else watching, not knowing what was happening, might consider reporting low-flying UFOs to the police!

For two hours, we followed Michelle through the fields and along the woods. Our early excitement faded as following the trail turned into hard work. We slipped and fell on patches of ice, we struggled over, under and through too many barbed-wire fences. I kept hoping Michelle would not charge through one of those fences and get cut.

At one point, we had to traverse steep drop-offs and get around impenetrable bushes. Thorns and swampy areas were a hazard, too. Where Michelle could glide from stone to stone over a swampy patch, we slipped and got wet. Where she could finesse through seemingly solid walls of four-foot-high undergrowth, we got entangled and tripped. Where she could skip effortlessly down steep ravines, we had to call her back while we worked our way around. More than once we found ourselves in precarious situations.

Then it happened. Following Michelle down into a ravine, we nearly fell off a rock ledge, a forty-foot fall that would have killed us. Equally frightening was the climb back up, steep and slippery.

Both Frank and I were exhausted now, and not a little scared. *Really scared* to be perfectly honest. This is the point in a search where I invariably ask myself, What the hell am I doing here? I should be sitting by the fire with cognac, not playing macho man. If I knew what I was doing, would I be standing on a rock ledge, soaking wet, chilled, bruised and scared to death? How could I have been stupid enough to get myself into this spot?

Of course, I didn't say all that out loud. All I said to Frank was, "Shit, now we have to climb back up."

"Should we rest first?" he suggested.

I decided we'd better not, we'd only get colder and stiffer. "Let's just take a few deep breaths and get the hell out of here," I said.

As usual, Frank had the perfect response, "T, if I die on the way back up, I forgive you."

I do not know how long it took us to get back up, nor do I know where or how Michelle got back up. What I do know is that even though I stopped smoking years ago, right then I needed a cigarette. As I paused to recover, I realized Michelle had been air scenting for quite some time. It was extremely unlikely Baker had walked this path, that much I knew. But I had no clue where Michelle left—or lost—the footpath and started air scenting. A major screwup on my part.

"Let's retrace our steps and find our way around this thing to keep heading in the direction we were going," I said. I couldn't say "our way back" because I had no idea which way "back" was. Nothing looked familiar. I was hoping Frank would agree and start heading in some direction, any direction. Then I could simply follow him while I got myself together.

"Which way, T?" he asked.

I sighed. "No clue." Then we both laughed and sat down.

"Time to regroup," said Frank. Boy, was he right. I promptly slid off the log I was sitting on to fall flat on my back in a pile of snow and leaves. That's when we both lost it. I hadn't laughed so hard since I was a kid in church and got the giggles during my First Holy Communion. But after the laughing and a few deep breaths, I began to get a grip.

OK, I thought to myself, we had our rock-climbing play break, we survived, but Baker is still out there and he's probably not very comfortable. We had been heading northeast, which I knew because, as always, I had been checking my compass every few minutes.

That's when I realized someone was missing: Michelle, here a moment ago, was nowhere to be seen. Now if I were a lay person, the urge would be to call or whistle. But I'm an SAR trainer—*so I waited to see what she was up to.* I always try to learn from my dog. The glow necklace can't hide for long and it didn't. Instead, as we moved northeast again, I saw Michelle waiting patiently. If she could have, she would have been tapping her foot impatiently. I marvel at her confidence, waiting and knowing that we would eventually come. "Willing" us to come.

"This way," I said to Frank at the sight of her glow necklace and her eyes reflecting in the starlight. With Michelle leading us, we picked and threaded our way around the gorge. According to the compass, we were shifting direction constantly. Still, Michelle was definitely going somewhere. I just couldn't be sure she was working. It was strange. She was walking at a pace so determined and fast that I had to run to keep up with her. Suddenly she swerved right, then made a ninety-degree turn to the left, broke into a run and disappeared.

"She found him!" said Frank.

"Let's go see." I was cautious. I had never seen her

respond to a "find" this way. Her behavior was missing something—intensity, excitement, something. We turned in the direction Michelle had disappeared and after a few minutes I could see the glow necklace. But her head was down, not moving, just sniffing.

That's when I knew that Michelle had found the dead body of our victim and she was acting subdued because it was a corpse. Much has been written and theorized about dogs' different responses to live and dead human finds. Are dogs depressed by finding a corpse? Or are they responding to the depression of their handlers who are often overwhelmed by tragedies such as earthquakes? This is a much-debated question that I've heard discussed many times.

As we got closer, I couldn't make out a body but I could see something reflecting. Then I heard it—running water. There was no corpse, Michelle just wanted a drink! No big deal—just going from momentary heart-pounding excitement to she's taking a drink. First I cursed, then I laughed. I should have remembered that she'd done this to me a couple times during mock searches. I should have remembered the deliberate but not intense body language. Still, my heart sank as I thought this entire diversion was just for water and had nothing to do with Baker. I waited as Michelle took a long slow drink then casually headed back to where we came from, making a left turn from where she had turned in for water and heading in the same direction we had been, northeast.

My poor heart regained its buoyancy and I felt hopeful again. Again Michelle seemed to be working, slow but methodical. Hell, we were all working slower, we were tired. I was also beginning to wonder how lost we might be. But then I figured if we backtracked southwest about the same distance we had come (calculating that distance by the time traveled), we'd be back where we had started and all we would have to do was head due south back to the road. But the thought of backtracking depressed me.

As we trudged over a patch of soggy terrain, I said to Frank, "She's still working, we're going to find this guy." My words sounded hollow to me, and all Frank did was grunt.

Another hour of stumbling behind Michelle. I hadn't looked at my compass for about an hour, so I checked and saw we were heading southeast. That concerned me, even frightened me a little. I signaled for a short rest to regroup, reminding myself how often I lecture on the folly of keeping on out of stubborn sheer will when it makes much more sense to stop and assess the situation. This was such a time. I just hoped it wasn't too late and we weren't totally lost.

Calling "Wait" to Michelle, we rested. I also wanted to write down the compass directions and times so we'd have a shot at backtracking if we had to.

This is where I wish Michelle had been taught "Take Me Back to Where We Started From," but no such luck. Nor did our R&R go well. As I reviewed the situation, too many negative thoughts crowded in. My chest tightened and my confidence in Michelle cracked.

Trust the dog, my ass. That old man didn't take this walk, he couldn't have crossed that terrain in his condition. Michelle can't be tracking him, she's air scenting. But maybe she's not air scenting. Maybe she lost the scent an hour ago and now she's led us into the middle of nowhere looking for it. Right about this time, I stopped thinking "search" and started thinking "survival."

Frank picked that moment to say, "T, save the water, I think we're going to die out here." His delivery was so perfect that I choked as I was drinking from my canteen, spewing water in his face as I exploded in laughter. Frank added that he thought the road was off to our right, east of us. I agreed that I thought we might have been paralleling the road.

Now I had a decision to make. Do we keep following Michelle or do we head back toward where we hope there is civilization? I had to decide if Michelle's body language was telling me that she still had occasional whiffs of scent or she was clueless. Was she following deer trails? Marion Hardy, one of the original American K-9 SAR handlers and one of the best, told me that it shouldn't happen with a properly trained dog, but sometimes on a long and arduous search a dog will "critter" out of frustration. When the dog can't find a human scent, they latch onto an animal's.

This was not an easy decision. What I really wanted to do was head back toward the road (as if we could find it!) because it was incomprehensible to me that Baker had walked this way and highly unlikely that Michelle could be air scenting him through these woods. But something wasn't quite right. When there is no scent at the start of a search, Michelle looks to me for a direction, then quarters the area in front of me to search for a scent. The problem at the moment? She was not looking to me for a direction—nor had she for a long time.

Trust the dog! Well, I wasn't sure I could do that. I knew I did not want to go deeper into the woods.

"What do you want to do?" asked Frank.

"Let's see what Michelle does." From the look on Frank's face and the defeated slouch in his shoulders, I must have sounded pretty doubtful myself.

Looking for Michelle to psyche her up to continue the search, I saw her marking a tree with her urine. A clue—she *might* be following an animal trail. And if she had gone in any other direction when I said, "Go find," I would have redirected her toward the road. But as it was she veered to the east—just where we wanted to go.

"Trust the dog," I said, more heartened.

"Bullshit," said Frank, "she wants civilization, too."

And so we meandered easterly for another hour until we broke out of the woods into a series of fields with a road on the far side. What a relief. Relief but no rest. Michelle continued forward at a brisk, deliberate pace. I couldn't believe it. Was it possible that she had been on the case the whole time, knowing exactly where she was going, closing in on the victim while I lost confidence?

When she got to the road, she turned left and continued in the same direction, duplicating the start of the search.

"Looks like she's still working," said Frank. And so we followed, paralleling the road for another quarter hour. Once again our trust was wavering. Why did she take us off the road, deep into the woods on that ridiculous journey, only to bring us back to the road?

As we came around a long left turn, a hill loomed ahead. It was small by Catskill Mountain standards but Mt. Everest by current Frank and Tom fatigue standards. We looked at each other.

"Oh shit," said Frank as Michelle started up, slow but

dogged. She was tired, too, and seemed glad when I called her back for a short rest. Our rest periods were coming closer and closer together now. Weather was a factor, too, as a raw wind had picked up. Keeping on the move meant keeping warm.

"How long do you think an old guy can last in this weather?" asked Frank. His question was a good adrenaline shot. We decided to radio Sheriff Adams before going any farther, to relay our location and to be sure the old man hadn't been found. The answer was negative.

We followed Michelle up a long, steep path bordered with grass and scrub. It was lighter now, the stars reflecting off patches of snow. I could see Michelle plainly, not just her glow necklace. I felt strange—my head was sweaty but my hands and feet were cold and I was chilled. For a passing moment, I had the urge to take off my hat with the miner's headlight, but I remembered I was on a search and needed to stay alert for clues.

We ascended for what felt like an eternity. Finally, we reached a point where we were more than weary, we were incredulous.

"No way," said Frank, "no way an old man with Parkinson's walked up this mountain."

"Maybe he didn't, maybe she's air scenting him." I wasn't sure if she was air scenting because she didn't move like she was; she really looked like she was trailing. But I had a hard time believing that. About four-fifths of the way to the summit, we stopped for another rest. I lay down, using my bump hat as a pillow, closed my eyes and said, "Don't wake me."

The next thing I knew Michelle was sitting on my

chest. I couldn't believe it. She stepped on my stomach, sat with her rear end in my face, and gave a deep sigh. I asked her if she'd like a cup of tea. Frank, of course, thought this was hilarious. I didn't mind the warmth and lay there until I couldn't breathe from her eighty pounds. When we were ready, I purposely turned downhill as I said, "Go find." She headed up.

"Trust the dog," I said with a hell of a lot less conviction than before.

"If she doesn't find this guy, I'm selling her to a Chinese restaurant for dog meat," said Frank. Another half hour and Michelle headed down the backside of the mountain toward a clearing that led into the woods. Dogs don't see peaks the way humans do. People will always stop at a summit as if it's some kind of accomplishment. Dogs don't even notice, they just keep on going.

Looking in the direction Michelle was heading was depressing—a rugged, steep descent down into oblivion. I asked Frank which direction he thought Baker's house might be from where we were standing. He pointed off to the right. As we looked in that direction, we saw light. We stared for a few seconds before we realized it was moving. And there was more than one—searchers! Foot searchers at the base of the mountain were heading up toward us.

"Thank goodness," I said, "they'll cover this side so we won't have to go down. I want to go to Hennessey's house and see if Michelle can pick up his track there. At this point, for all I know Michelle could be keying in on those searchers. After all, it's been hours since she smelled the scent article. Let's scent on the pillow again and see if she can latch onto the route he took when he left his house."

I remember feeling very pleased with that idea—it seemed a lot better than continuing on this wild-goose chase. Still, it took us an hour to get back down the mountain to the road, get picked up by Adams and taken to Baker's house. On the way, I told Adams that Michelle may have been scenting the other searchers in lieu of Baker.

His home was tucked neatly into the woods, a real country cottage. I left Michelle in the car while I questioned Mrs. Baker and her relatives. I wanted Michelle to get a few minutes' rest but I also knew it would be easier to psyche her up if she had been contained for a while.

But Mrs. Baker had nothing new to add, and my questions only served to make her more concerned. Finally, I got the pillow from the car trunk and, placing it in a strategic spot outside the house, called Michelle from the car. First, I brought her into the cottage, which she checked out with a fair degree of intensity. Then, with Sheriff Adams, Frank and the entire Baker family standing alongside us, I had her scent off the pillow and said, "Go find!"

Boy, do I love that dog! After pushing her nose into every person standing there, causing a succession of squeals, grunts and giggles, she headed off in the direction Baker had taken when he left the house.

Thirty minutes later, as we were going along the road, Michelle cut ninety degrees to the right of a harvested cornfield. It was obvious she was air scenting, her nose high and quartering back and forth, sometimes sprinting, sometimes stopping dead as if she'd lost it. Excited at first, my enthusiasm waned as this went on for a time with no real direction chosen.

I tried working her into the wind but it died. I'm pretty good at telling wind direction with my face, the face being much more sensitive than a wet finger held to the wind. Not even the flame from my Bic would flutter. Frustrating. Finally, after another hour, Frank pointed out it was nearly daybreak. "We should get some rest and continue in the daylight," he said.

"But the guy may freeze to death while we're sleeping," I said.

"We're accomplishing nothing but using up all our reserves," said Frank. "We're too tired to make an intelligent decision and, besides, Michelle also needs a rest."

He was right. I felt a tremendous wave of fatigue as I entertained the thought of actually lying down. I radioed Adams that we needed a rest and he directed us to a firehouse nearby where we could crash. Lying on the cot, I closed my eyes only to see woods, rocks and a floating glow necklace. I was totally exhausted yet wide awake.

"Would you shut up," said Frank.

"Shut up? I didn't say anything."

"You keep sighing."

I felt like crying—for the old man freezing, maybe dying, for the frustration of not finding him.

"Come on, T," said Frank, aware of my despair, "for all we know he may have had a heart attack and died eight hours ago. Or maybe he's at a friend's house sleeping and his wife forgot he wasn't coming home. You know how these things go. Stop beating yourself up, you're doing the best you can."

"Frank, I really blew it taking you along as my co-op." I was trying to be funny, but Frank didn't answer. Within minutes I heard him snoring softly. Still, I lay there awake. The greatest fear a K-9 searcher has is that the lost victim will die in your search grid, that you will fail to find him. After a long drink, Michelle curled up on my jacket, which I had put down for her as a bed. She gave a couple big sighs and then I heard her snoring softly, too.

I was deep into a dream of being lost at sea when an ocean liner's whistle shrieked in my ear. I woke up with a jolt to find it was the phone in the firehouse. Frank shuffled over to answer it. When he hung up, it took a long time for the message to sink in.

"What?" I said it again and again as he spoke.

"—helicopter spotted him . . . he spent the night curled up with his dog . . . mild exposure but OK. . . ."

"He's alive? Oh thank you, God. Why didn't someone tell us he had a dog!" Still, relief rushed through me. If he hadn't survived, I would have carried that guilt for the rest of my life. I may talk intellectual but I live emotional.

The aftermath was not pleasant. I felt like shit. Bottom line: We didn't find him. Fact: During a K-9 search almost all errors are handler errors. This was one of those times.

The helicopter spotted Baker just over a rise at the edge of a wood on the side of a mountain. *The location was less than five hundred yards from where I turned Michelle around after we saw the searchers' lights in the distance. I failed to trust the dog.*

*   *   *

Here is what really happened:
Baker did cross the street because he knew about the horses and enjoyed looking at them. Then he crossed back and followed the road until he got to some fields he thought would be a shortcut home. The snow squall left him disoriented, especially after the snow fell and covered any landmarks. So he found his way back to the road and continued until he saw the mountain and tried another shortcut. Michelle took us along that same path. The snow squall did something to the scent particles but she eventually air scented her way back to the road and his trail. She never lost it.

Thinking back, I wince. Michelle never once wavered in her consistent pace. When she made that sharp turn off the road and up the mountain, we knew she was working. We didn't hesitate to follow. And when I turned her around, she had still been moving with that same deliberate intent. Nothing like hindsight to make you feel stupid. And a yelp I heard her make when she went through the barbed-wire fence? When we woke up at the firehouse, she was lying in a pool of dried blood. She had raked her belly, but never once complained. Marking with her urine? Baker's dog. It all made sense now.

But I lost my trust in Michelle. Blame it on impatience, blame it on lack of experience. I'm older now with many more searches under my belt. I'm certainly more patient. Most important—Baker lived.

Training Notes

*How a Reject Labrador Retriever
Became an Extraordinary Hero*

I received a call one day to train a year-old black lab whose hip displasia had caused her to be rejected from a training program for Seeing Eye dogs. Her name was Lady and she had been adopted by a family with a young autistic child, a six-year-old named Lisa.

From the moment I arrived at the family's home where I would do the training, I could see that Lady was an exceptionally bright subject. In fact, it took only three lessons to turn her into a well-mannered cooperative dog. She was so good that I found myself encouraging her owner to teach Lady new commands.

"She's too smart and tuned in and anxious to please," I said. "She'll get bored with heel, sit, stay, down and come. She'll create her own games if you don't keep her stimulated."

One of the pitfalls of dog training is boring the dog into misbehaving simply by being too repetitious and not creative enough. But another dynamic was happening here, too. It's best explained if I make the point that when you train a dog, you are also being trained by the dog. Take Michelle, for example. She teaches me the best way to teach her through her responses to me; by observing her responses carefully I'm able to improve my body language, heighten my sensitivity to her and increase my patience. As Michelle is patient with me, so am I with her.

I was mulling all this over while deciding what to do next with Lady. Using Michelle as a foil, I asked myself, What makes Michelle happy? Easy answer: working. Michelle's specialty is finding people and she is never bored while searching for a human being.

Then it hit me: Lady is a retriever—she will be happiest when working as a retriever, and retrieving includes searching. I'll teach her to "find" Lisa!

I had some understanding of autism through my wife, Jaye, who, as a speech therapist, has been working with autistic children for over twenty years. I realized that Lady's wonderful temperament, which could have made her an excellent Seeing Eye dog, could also make her excellent with an autistic child— somehow.

Lady had come into their house already sensitive, soft, smart and cooperative. She smiled the day we first met and I remember thinking she had the most beautiful and wise eyes I had ever seen in a dog. One look at Lady and I'd felt privileged to be working with her.

So I knew we could do this. Especially because I

had had the time to observe the interaction between Lisa and Lady, and Lady treated Lisa differently. Where she would happily roughhouse with the parents when invited, she was extremely respectful of Lisa's "space."

I'm very tuned in to how dogs use physical contact with people. Michelle has taught me a great deal about this with everything from body slams in play to gently touching the inside of my hand with her wet nose to signal that she's found something I've touched with my hand. Because of my awareness of the many levels of body language communication with my dog, I was acutely aware of how Lady looked to make gentle physical contact with Lisa but would back off at the slightest sign Lisa had had enough. It was as if Lady was a born therapist!

When I proposed the possibility of training Lady to find Lisa, Lisa's mother was intrigued. "Do you mean that if I turned my back and Lisa had disappeared somewhere inside or outside the house that Lady could find her?"

"You betcha."

"That would be incredible," she said.

We got started. First, Lady had to be taught the concept of find, starting with a visual and graduating to the nose. We used "runaways" where I would hold Lady back while Lisa's mother made silly noises and gestures and then ran to hide behind a tree. Lady, watching the whole time, would be psyched by me. I would hold her back and keep urging her in an excited voice if "she wanted to work." While she is bursting with excitement, strange noises are still coming from behind the tree—then I release her and say,

"Go find Mom!" And so we worked, eventually progressing to where Lady could not see where her target was but would have to use her nose to find Lisa's mom.

You may recall from earlier that a human has five million olfactory cells in their nose but a dog like Lady has one hundred million! If Lady can smell the bones of a decomposed victim ninety feet underwater, she could certainly smell Lisa's mom. I just had to teach her to tell me *when* she smelled her.

To do that we worked on teaching Lady to smell three different ways—tracking, air scenting and trailing. Tracking is following the actual path walked; air scenting is picking up a human's scent particles in the air or from a scent pool; and trailing is a combination of the two.

Once she had mastered her tracking, air scenting and trailing of Lisa's mom, I had to teach her to find me at the mother's command. Ultimately, it would be the mother who would command Lady to find Lisa. To accomplish that we had one final, critical challenge: teach Lady to find Lisa without Lisa's encouragement or participation.

This was critical because Lisa would not be praising Lady for her work. The training was complicated, too, by the fact that Lisa was often hostile to the rest of us. I tackled the problem by teaching Lady to find Lisa with the use of a clean scent article. I explained to the family that the article could have no one else's scent except Lisa's. Lady was quick to pick up on this concept, which led me to another idea, the creation of a new and very pragmatic command—"Escort Lisa."

The command meant that Lady should stay with

Lisa no matter where she went or what she did, even if Lisa shouted for Lady to go away or threw things at her. This would be enormously valuable to the family because it meant that if Lisa somehow got away from adult supervision, Lady would be there. Also, one of the hallmarks of autism is a fear of entering new environments, like moving from room to room, alone. If Lisa could enter a room with familiar Lady at her side, the risk of anxiety would be significantly diminished.

It all worked. Today, Lisa and Lady have their own unique friendship. Lady's presence is not only soothing and lovingly therapeutic for Lisa, but Lady is totally understanding and forgiving of Lisa's moods. She is always happiest in Lisa's presence *because she is working.*

Meanwhile, Mom and Dad have a wonderful therapist who never calls in sick, is always in a good mood, works 24/7, is a therapist to them as well—and never complains!

And so it was that Lady's story ended up in a wonderful, interesting book, *Everyday Heroes, Extraordinary Dogs* by Sherry Bennett Warshauer.

2

A Halloween Search

This search started with a twist so surreal, Frank and I couldn't believe it even as we stood there. "There" was a cemetery, the time was midnight, the day was Halloween and we were under a full moon!

"Can you believe this scene, man?" said Frank as he looked up at the sky. He didn't have to add what we were both thinking: this was one spooky situation. Following his gaze up, a chill ran down my back. The luminous moon kept disappearing, hidden by clouds that rushed by like dark, driven demons. What a perfect night for ghosts and goblins.

"If I see a witch on a broom fly by, I'm outta here," said Frank. "Let someone else find the escapee.

"What are *we* doing here anyway, T? This isn't a lost child or some oldster with Alzheimer's—this is a sixteen-year-old running away from reform school. Hell, he could be us some years back."

"More likely you!" I aimed for humor but what I felt was less a chuckle than a shiver. Frank was right. We never planned to chase criminals with our dogs, we wanted to save lives.

It was Ed who had called me at home about the missing boy. The target of the search was a sixteen-year-old runaway named Don who had been missing since ten o'clock that night from the correctional facility. He thought it was a good idea if Frank and I, two-thirds of the Amigo K-9 Search and Rescue Unit, helped out with the search. Ed and his dog, Abu, were the other third of our Amigo team, but they couldn't join us.

"We're way understaffed tonight," Ed had explained. "Two other staffers are out sick so there's no way I can join you with Abu. Take Michelle—it'll be great practice—she'll be looking for someone *who doesn't want to be found*."

He had a point there. As we spoke on the phone, I looked down at my Michelle. She was whining softly and prancing around, reminding me of a spring coil wound too tight. Not quite a year old, Michelle was still in SAR training. She had not yet been officially certified as a search-and-rescue dog. Still, she was the only "working" dog in town. Frank's Bernese mountain dog, Yogi, was not as advanced as Michelle, as he was still in the early stages of training.

It was shortly after 11 P.M. when Ed called back. "I've got a clean scent article and a PLS so meet me at the church across from the cemetery in thirty minutes. I'll give you the scent article and show you where Don was last seen."

"Is the kid dangerous?" I asked. After all, another name for Ed's place of employment was "reform school."

"You mean armed? Nah . . . he's a punk, bluster and hot air." Ed said that about everyone. "Meet me in exactly thirty minutes," he said.

So that's how we ended up—me, Michelle and Frank—at the edge of the cemetery under conditions perfect for a horror film. Except for the temperature, which was very cold. The ground around the graves was covered with a dusting of frost. Some stretches sparkled with moonlight, others were dark, murky pools. None were inviting.

"Feels colder than the twenty-five degrees I heard on the radio." Frank sounded very hesitant. "Oh well, let's do it, T, you're the one who said, 'Real adventures always include some fear.' "

"Bull, Frank—*you* said that."

As I spoke, Frank was already heading for the PLS. I followed with the scent article, a sweatband in a plastic bag. Ed had insisted it was "clean," untouched by anyone except Don and Ed. The sweatband had come off the boy's head after he worked out. It would be rich with scent particles from his hair and sweat as well as fumes from his mouth and nose. Ed had handed me the bag as we all huddled together, so Michelle got to sniff it while standing with us, hopefully zeroing in on the scent of the one person who wasn't there.

Michelle knows the routine. Now she was wired. Fact is, she knew what was happening the moment I hung up the phone and reached for my SAR vest. From that point on, she did not take her eyes off me. That, too, is a preliminary stage of a search.

She looks to establish eye contact with me. Not a dominant eye contact but a concerned, questioning look. The question is "When do I go to work?" and the concern in her expression is how she tells me she's on full alert, ready to respond the instant I command. And at a time like this, the word *command* takes on new meaning. Michelle is so excited and intense in anticipation of the imminent search that she becomes overly sensitive to my body language and voice intonations, looking to use anything I say or do as an excuse to tear out of there and start searching.

Her impatience may be especially heightened because of her youth, but it is matched by my coolness. My goal is to keep her keeping herself under control while, at the same time, subtly stoking her desire to work. I want her ready to burst with energy and intensity when I finally say, "Go find." Until then, however, I appear to ignore her while getting everything ready. Every once in a while, I throw a glance her way, make eye contact and softly mouth the words "going to work soon," but then I look away and continue preparing. The preparations are adjusting the SAR vest, filling the canteen and other moves that Michelle recognizes as prep for a search. As I do these things, her intensity continues to ratchet up.

From the point that she hears "Go find" and explodes into action, I am telling her to pace herself, to dole out the intensity with control, to avoid enthusiasm burnout.

Donald McCaig, a respected dog trainer and author, wrote that "control is a gift, fine control is a delicate grip on chaos." I never really understood that until Michelle and I trained each other. He was talking about border collies but the same goes for search dogs. While Michelle is often working out of my sight and making many independent decisions, it is our training together that reinforces my control over her. This control, delicate yet firm, is the thread that binds us even when we can't see one another.

I caught up to Frank at the spot that Ed said was the PLS, two stone pillars that seemed to serve as an entrance to the graveyard. No standing on ceremony for Michelle—she tore into the graveyard at a gallop.

"And without further ado," said Frank, grinning at me. Then he started to follow Michelle into the sea of headstones. I waved him back.

"We do it by the book," I said and called Michelle back to us. She came begrudgingly, prancing and whining with impatience. Holding the bag with Don's headband close to the spot on the ground where the boy was last seen, I opened it and Michelle, without being told, shoved her nose inside. She grabbed the headband between her teeth and turned so abruptly that she knocked the bag out of my hands as she headed back into the cemetery.

"Aren't you supposed to say, 'Go find'?" said Frank as we both wheeled around to watch Michelle.

"Call her an extremely enthusiastic trainee," I said as I ran after Michelle. Then I slowed and said, "Whoa, running is a no-no, Frank. She'll check back with us— she just needs an energy release."

Instead, we walked briskly after Michelle. By not running, we were able to become more aware of our surroundings, especially the silence. The silence was particularly striking in the cold clear air as we walked among the graves and headstones. We slowed down to avoid accidentally kicking or stumbling over any of the older headstones, which looked as if they might break. The clouds skittering over the moon made it hard to see, and more than once we stumbled.

Then one ancient gravestone toppled over after Frank bumped into it accidentally. We were trying to right it for the second time when it cracked in half at the very instant that we heard a shriek, followed by a baby's cry, from the woods off to our right.

"Jeez!" I stumbled backward, almost knocking over another stone. The shriek and cry had lasted less than two seconds but we knew what made that sound. We knew it because we had heard an identical cry very recently during a barbecue at Ed's house.

It was late September and half a dozen couples had all been sitting around a bonfire out in a field, everyone quietly enjoying the peace and beauty of a starry night when the velvet silence was torn by that same horrible shriek and cry. As we all scrambled to our feet, looking around in surprise, several people on the far side of the fire backed away suddenly. A dog had entered the ring of light around the fire. It was a malamute mix that belonged to one of the couples, but that animal looked more like a wolf as she approached us from the shadows with furtive steps, her head down and stretched forward. What had everyone backing up so fast was the corpse hanging from her jaws—a dead baby rabbit. Her owners explained that their pet had a habit of hunting the critters, and when they're killed "baby rabbits sound that way." So Frank and I knew exactly what creature had made that awful sound coming from the woods off to the right of the cemetery.

"That's one baby rabbit that won't know the stresses of adulthood," quipped my buddy.

"Aren't you Monsieur Sympathy," I said, my heart still pounding a little.

"Would you like to say a few words for our dearly departed little rodent before we continue our search?" Frank delivered his remark in a perfect Irish brogue.

I refused to let him see my smile and instead looked around for Michelle. I had put two glow necklaces around her neck but could see no sign of the neon rings. I scanned the graveyard in the direction we were headed. After a short while, I caught sight of her, the orange glow necklaces moving jerkily near the far edge of the cemetery off to our right.

"What do you think killed the rabbit?" I asked as we moved toward Michelle.

"Rabbits are meat for a lot of animals in woods like these," said Frank. "Could be anything from a hawk to a bear."

"Oh yeah? What's between a hawk and a bear?" I asked as I stepped carefully around a grave. I was trying to avoid trampling on anything sacred but having a hard time without a flashlight. This was one of those frustrating situations where a flashlight would be too much but no flashlight was too little.

Frank ignored my question, saying, "Two days ago a friend told me he came face-to-face with a rabid dog. Said it was pretty scary—the dog was very big, mangy and threatening. But just when he was expecting to be attacked the dog walked away. He was pretty unnerved and called the police about it. They said they'd had reports of rabid animals around here recently, a coyote and a fox. So, you know, a rabbit's a nice meal for any one of those guys, not to mention a bobcat or a mountain lion—"

"Mountain lion! Don't give me that crap, Frank, there's no mountain lion around here." My voice bellowed in the cemetery silence.

"Yeah there is," he insisted. "This is real mountains, T-man, this ain't no suburbia." Then Frank said another friend of his, a bow hunter, had seen one.

"You remember Art, you met him at my house last summer," said Frank. "He said last bow season he either saw three of them or the same one three times. Scared him, he felt like he was being stalked. Like he was the hunted, not the hunter. After seeing the lion for the third time, he got so paranoid that he was convinced he was being hunted. He became acutely aware that all he had was a bow and arrow. The mountain lion had the advantage—muscle and stealth. After the third sighting, Art was so rattled, he cut his trip short by two days.

"T, I'm the only guy he told the real story to. Everyone else was told that he and the lion stalked each other until Art had to go back to work. But he told me the lion scared the hell out of him, he couldn't wait to get out of the woods. So believe me, T, we got mountain lions in these woods."

By now Frank and I were moving along at a pace that was pretty brisk for the conditions, both of us breathing hard. I mulled over his story as I kept an eye out for my dog.

"You see Michelle?" asked Frank.

"Huh-uh." I exhaled. I'd been looking for her for a while, and though I had fleeting glimpses of the iridescent orange rings floating between headstones in the distance, the last sighting was some time ago. Now there was no sign of her.

"You think she might be out of the cemetery? She was near the edge before."

"What's out there past the cemetery?" I asked

"A big field with a huge equipment barn at the far end that's surrounded by woods."

"What kind of—?" Just then I saw Michelle. I had been looking so far into the distance that I was startled when she suddenly appeared just fifty feet away and coming at me. She had something in her mouth. Running up, she stopped to drop it a few feet away. Hard as I've tried, she refuses to drop immediately in front of me, always a few feet away.

"It's an article find, Frank, probably something dropped by Don."

The find was a slightly used pack of matches. As I picked it up, Michelle whined.

"Show me," I said immediately.

The command "Show me" tells her "show me where you found it," and is a "refind" command. In contrast, if Michelle had come to me with a stick in her mouth or had come back to me and then picked up a stick, it would be her way of telling me that she found the missing human being.

This is a critical part of search training because a dog could find a person a quarter mile away and consider the job done. Or an unconscious child could be thirty-five feet away but hidden under leaves; unless the dog brings you right to the victim, you may never make the find. The real working search dog's job consists of two major steps: one, find the person; two, hook you up with the find.

With what I know now I would have trained Michelle differently on an article find. I should not have trained her to bring me the article, but rather to alert me to the existence of the article and then *bring me to it* without her disturbing the scene, especially if it's a potential crime scene. But I didn't know any better back then, and it was much easier and more fun to train her to retrieve things.

As soon as I said, "Show me," Michelle wheeled around to head back out through the headstones with Frank and myself close behind. But before she turned, she had touched her nose to the bag with Nick's sweatband that was hanging from my belt.

"Man, she's good—did you see her connect those matches to Nick? I hope you appreciate my being here to point these things out to you, T. Someday you'll realize just how valuable I am," said Frank, huffing and puffing as we ran after Michelle.

Grinning from ear to ear, I was too proud and excited to think up a good comeback. I was too pleased with how beautifully Michelle was working and too excited by the fact that we were closing in on this kid who didn't want to be found.

In a few minutes, we were approaching the far right corner of the cemetery, the location where Michelle had been lingering when we spotted her from afar. She was sniffing all over the place but sat down as we got near. I had trained her to sit in front of the spot where she had found an article as her way of indicating the location. She didn't hold the sit as long as she was supposed to; she was much too excited and eager to continue. What she is supposed to do is sit and wait while I investigate the scene for any other clues. As carefully as we could without trampling the place, Frank and I used our flashlights to scour the area for any other signs of Don. Meanwhile, Michelle kept whining and trying to start for the field.

I held her back with commands. According to the rules, I was to thoroughly investigate the area, radio in whatever I found, then continue the search. The reality of the situation was that not only was there no one to call, we didn't have radios on us (an amateurish oversight committed by all of us), and Michelle was telling us in no uncertain terms to stop wasting time because she was hot on the trail.

The situation was not the easiest to manage. Michelle's behavior of darting around the area and snorting made it clear that Don had stopped here and in so doing had created a scent pool that she was keying on. She needed to be praised for this, but every time I praised her, I found myself calling her back too much or discouraging her when she was doing her job so well.

At the same time, we were looking for a fugitive but making our position too obvious with all the flashlights and activity. If we were looking for a lost person who wanted to be found, that would be fine, but under the circumstances I felt like a sitting duck under a spotlight.

I was also worried for Michelle—she doesn't know the meaning of "bad guys." All her training had involved victims who praised her and loved her when they were found. She wasn't trained to find a criminal who would hate her, might even try to harm her. A search dog that is seriously hurt or scared by a "victim" can easily be ruined as a search dog. At the same time, Michelle was no wimp and I knew from experience that she was less likely to be frightened than turned on and excited by a threatening response. That was the Doberman in her. Still, I didn't want to put her at risk.

So I was standing in one spot, dealing with this dilemma, when Frank said, "Hey, look at this!" He was standing about twenty feet away in an area that Michelle was sniffing at intently.

"Hold it right there and shine your light," said Frank as I walked toward him. It was quite a scene: a crushed Marlboro pack, a fresh cigarette butt, several footprints on a small patch of snow and, best of all, a urine stain that was brought to our attention by Michelle with her sniffing and whining. Though the whining got our attention, it was when she peed on the spot that I examined it more closely. It wasn't her regular pee, it was a marking pee. When she's marking an area she lifts her leg, though not as high as a male dog. It was obvious she was deliberately marking that spot.

"Well, looky here," I said, triumph in my voice. "Our man didn't stop to have a cigarette, he stopped to take a leak and decided to have a smoke while he was at it."

"That makes more sense for someone on the run," said Frank. "Also shows no respect for the dead."

"Look who's talking—you've trampled more stuff in here than a drunken elephant."

"At least I'm remorseful," said Frank.

"Right!" I snorted.

"I s'pose you think you looked like a ballet dancer," Frank countered. We kept up our banter as we followed Michelle, who was still working out of the graveyard and off to the right.

We were now in what appeared to be an endless field. Michelle was quartering in front of us, working the scent cone. I was excited by her actions and pointed it out to

Frank. "Look, she's working the wind, she's got his scent, we're going to find this kid."

"Yeah? Then what happens when we find him and he doesn't want to go back?"

That was a very good question and one that had been in the back of my mind for some time. There was a strong likelihood that the boy would refuse to come with us, leaving us with few options. We couldn't call anyone because we didn't have radios—but we did have flares. Also, I had already figured that I could use the threat of "Michelle the Doberman" to intimidate him into cooperating. Then Frank could go for help while Michelle and I "guarded" Don. All this was hypothetical because Michelle wasn't trained for any of that, but I figured we could bluff it.

Suddenly, from somewhere in the woods, we heard a bloodcurdling scream.

"Jee-sus!" I said. I happened to be looking at Michelle at that moment and saw her jump in shock. Then she growled and barked, working her way back to us. For a few seconds, she stood against my leg for support. She was startled, frightened, angry and protective. I petted her and with each stroke she growled louder in the direction of the sound, gaining bravado from my support.

Neither Frank nor I had ever heard that sound before, but we knew exactly what it was. We stood absolutely frozen to the ground. Never had I felt so vulnerable as I did that night in the middle of a field in the middle of nowhere listening to the roar of a mountain lion.

My eyes searched the edge of the wood in desperation but I saw nothing. I think I would have had a heart attack if that mountain lion had emerged from the woods and headed toward us. I wondered if Michelle had an instinctive knowledge handed down from her wolf ancestors. Did she have any idea how dangerous that animal was? Did she care?

I don't know how long we stood there before Frank said something, which I don't remember. I just remember trying to do some relaxation breathing, but instead I was hyperventilating. Finally, I heard him.

"You there, man?"

"No, definitely not, Frank. I'm on a beach in the Caribbean and this is a dream. Tell me this is a dream, Frank. Tell me I didn't just hear a mountain lion."

Frank was grinning as he said, "Don't be ridiculous—that was an owl. A good omen according to the Indians, or maybe a bad one, I'm not sure. What do we do now?"

"You mean an Indian from Bombay or an Apache?"

"What? Bombay, Apache? What are you talking about?" Frank looked confused.

"The Indian omen—what kind of Indian?"

"A wooden Indian, Tom. I repeat—now what do we do?"

My mind was racing. We had two options. Continue the search in spite of the scream, or discontinue because of the scream. The more I thought about it, I knew quitting wasn't an option. We don't quit. Plus, I knew we were very close to finding Don, and Michelle was raring to go. There was a subtext, too—Frank would never let me forget it if we quit.

So the question was how to proceed in light of a possible big cat in the woods?

"Frank," I said, "you take Michelle and find Don while I use my tracking skills to find the mountain lion and kill it. Then we use our flares to find each other and return as conquering heroes."

"No way, man," whined Frank, "you always get to do

the good stuff. I'll get the lion and you take Michelle and find the kid."

"OK, Michelle wouldn't work for you anyhow."

Our mood lightened by the banter, we were now silent. Pondering.

"The great likelihood is that the lion will avoid man, but that's no guarantee," said Frank. "It could be hungry enough to find us worth investigating, and if Michelle finds the lion that's bad news for Michelle. Hell, it could be a mother with cubs nearby and that's even more dangerous!"

He was right. Michelle was in more danger than either of us. A lion was not going to be very interested in two men jumping around and lighting flares—but cornered by a dog? She would fight.

Then Frank hit the mark: "Would Michelle listen if she found the lion and you told her to 'Leave It'?"

I thought about that. The only similar experience I'd had with Michelle was when deer crossed her path right in the middle of her working a trail. Her response was always the same. She would bolt after the deer while I was screaming "Leave it," continue after the deer for about twenty-five feet, then return sheepishly and resume her search. I never considered it much of a problem because she wasn't really crittering, which is when a dog chases animals instead of people. She just had a spot of a different kind of fun for a few minutes. But this was different. The deer were always swifter and running away. A mountain lion doesn't run like a deer, and what if that lion is protecting young ones?

"I'm going to put Michelle on a harness with a forty-foot line, that way I can keep her out of harm's way," I said to Frank as I removed my SAR vest. I had never done this with her before. Technically, she would not be allowed to raise her nose to the wind to air scent while in-harness. Instead, she would be required to keep her nose to the ground following the actual track taken by the victim/target.

I spoke to her as I put the harness on, as much for Frank's sake as Michelle's. "Life has many variables and exceptions, Michelle. If you find the actual footpath, great, but you can air scent all you want and it's OK with me, just *find* the kid and I'll be happy. If you—I mean *when* you *find* the kid, the harness will keep you safe should he have bad intentions, not to mention Mr. Lion. So forgive me for the change in our routine but it's good for you to learn to adjust and adapt to sudden changes. And if you don't like it, tough. Let's *find* him!" I emphasized *find* several times to get her restarted with enthusiasm.

She was off and pulling so fast and hard that I had trouble holding the leash while I got my SAR vest back on. I didn't want to discourage her so there I went, half running, half dragging, while trying to get my arm in the damn vest. Frank trotted next to me, helping me dress and laughing. Finally I was able to slow Michelle to a fast walk.

She was headed in the same direction she had been before the lion's roar, working across the middle of the field with the woods off to the right and the road along the cemetery to our left. Frank and I kept conversation to a minimum, and when we did talk, we whispered because Michelle's body language and pulling intensity signaled we were closing in. We didn't want to telegraph our arrival or miss any sounds from the boy—not to mention the lion. In retrospect, we were listening most intently for the lion.

After a short time, the dark outline of the equipment barn loomed off to our right, along the edge of the forest. The shifting shadows of the moon gave it an ominous presence. Michelle was pulling so hard now that my back was aching and my hands were tired and sore, even through my gloves. As we approached the barn, she dragged us right toward a large swinging door, which was held shut with a crossbar through U brackets. She jumped at the door, barking in frustration.

"Quiet!" said Frank and I simultaneously. Then I praised her and said, "Wait." Michelle whined impatiently, prancing in place, while Frank and I had a hurried discussion.

"He's in there," I said softly.

Frank leaned to whisper in my ear, "How did he close the door like this from the inside?"

"He must have gotten in somewhere else, but he's in there. Trust the dog."

"OK—how do you want to handle it?"

"Let's go right in and tell him to come out. Maybe we'll get lucky," I said.

With that, Frank slid the crossbar out of the brackets and pulled the door open, saying, "You go left and I'll go right." We entered fast, crouching. Frank moved to the right and I moved left, our flashlights quartering the area as we looked for the boy.

"The game's over, Don," I said as I held Michelle tight. She was chafing at the bit and hard to contain. Frank still kids me about that little announcement, alleging it was more of a squeak than an order. He's probably right—I remember the moment and how my heart was pounding so hard I could barely hear myself.

Seconds passed. No response. Dead silence. Even Michelle was still as our flashlights probed the darkness. The place was real spooky with tractors, fifty-gallon drums and other farm equipment creating suspicious-looking shadows. "Over there . . . over there . . . try there," we continued to whisper as we illuminated everything that looked like a lurking figure.

Suddenly Frank bellowed, "If we let the dog loose, she'll find you in a second and, believe me, you don't want that!" All hell broke loose then as Michelle started barking wildly and leaped forward, yanking the leash right out of my surprised hands. She disappeared into a maze of machinery and tools.

Dashing after her, we were stopped by the sound of the huge barn door slamming shut and the crossbar sliding in place to lock it. Torn for a moment as to which way to go, we opted to follow Michelle's loud incessant barking. As we stumbled through the obstacle course in the barn, I wondered if there were two escapees. If Michelle had cornered one, who closed the door on us?

I saw the leash before I saw Michelle. It was wedged under a piece of equipment. Now I knew her barking was her frustration at being stuck, not a find. After I freed the leash, she brought us to an open window five fcct off thc floor.

"I'll do the window and come around and open the door," said Frank, heading that way.

I grabbed his jacket and pulled him back. "No time for that. Michelle tracks him right from here, right now." And with that I hoisted Michelle up to the window ledge and let out enough leash for her to jump to the ground. Frank and I followed.

We had exited through the rear of the barn and Michelle now made a ninety-degree turn and headed into the woods, which were bordered, to our dismay, with a mess of thorny undergrowth, slush and rotted wood. Michelle dragged us forward for what seemed a very long time. I let her have only about ten feet of leash, more concerned than ever for her safety now that the boy had demonstrated a definite lack of cooperation.

Then Michelle turned right, heading deeper into the woods. Even though we had surer footing now, I had another concern: getting lost. As we ran, I asked Frank to take a compass reading every two minutes so we would be able to find our way out. We had entered an area of old growth with large trees and much easier walking. Actually, we were jogging now as Michelle was chafing at the bit again. We were closing in on Don.

"We're heading pretty much due west," said Frank after about ten minutes. We were both breathing hard, rasping as we spoke. "When we see him," huffed Frank, "I'm going to take him down and end this." This was not just macho talk. Frank is a black belt who came in second in the open karate finals at Madison Square Garden—more than capable of taking someone down.

"I'll be right there to back you up," I said, huffing, "unless, of course, he's really tough."

Our pace was now too fast and exhausting to keep talking. As the chase wore on, I realized I needed to slow down and pace myself. That kid may have youth and fear propelling him, I thought, but he smokes. With Frank's karate and bicycle riding and my jogging, we're in excellent condition, so if we just persevere, we'll get him.

Fifteen minutes later, drenched in sweat under my

heavy jacket, I had to ask myself, Who am I kidding? How are we ever going to catch a sixteen-year-old traveling light? After all, when I was that age I could easily outrun two forty-something guys.

Michelle kept us going. She was pulling as hard as ever. "We've turned south again," Frank rasped.

"Note the time and jot it down." I was just reaching my limit when Michelle started to slow. In spite of the better pace, which was a relief, I felt bone tired. But that feeling vanished in an instant with the sudden signal that Michelle had a find.

Her hackles went rigid, she swept to the right, growling as she pulled us through a clump of trees to the edge of a clearing. Suddenly she froze and let out a horrible snarl. The sound was so shocking, I stumbled back in surprise.

"Oh, no," said Frank under his breath.

In the center of the clearing, standing six feet above us on a downed tree, was the mountain lion. A large female, her green eyes were riveted on us. She spat at the beam from my flashlight, showing two rows of long white teeth. Then starting with a low gurgle, she launched a growl that escalated to a scream. A terrifying noise that made me feel like every cell and molecule in my body had disassociated. I had the weirdest understanding in that instant of what Captain Kirk meant when he said, "Beam me up, Scotty."

Over the next few moments, Michelle did something that I think saved our lives. She lunged forward—not at the lion but in front of Frank and me. She was not giving chase but communicating, "They're with me. If you want them, you have to go through me first!"

The cat focused piercing green eyes on Michelle and

opened its mouth to give another hair-raising scream. Light reflected off droplets of saliva flying through the air. Michelle responded by planting her feet, puffing out her chest and intensifying her snarl. Her courage inspired me to action. One thing I know is the importance of the departure in preventing aggression from an animal. If you run, you will be perceived as prey and probably precipitate an attack.

With that in mind, Frank and I moved in tandem, slowly backing away and taking care not to stumble. Any sudden movement could be disastrous. Michelle knew not to turn her back on the lion. At my urging, she backed away slowly, still snarling.

The lion watched us, transfixed by our retreat. We were still backing away when she suddenly leapt from the tree and disappeared.

"You think she's gone? Like as far away from us as possible?" asked Frank, hope in his voice.

I couldn't be sure. The very fact she had let us find her unnerved me.

"She can't surprise us with Michelle here," was the best I could answer. "We can watch our backs anyway."

"Over there," Frank said, gesturing toward a large boulder. I knew what he meant; it was a place where we could regroup in safety. The rock had a flat top and was set far enough away from trees and bushes that we would have a decent lookout while we rested.

And so we sat, the three of us, back to back to back.

No one uttered a sound. We weren't relaxing, we were listening. What we needed was silence—silence meaning no sound from the lion. But as we listened, the woods seemed too quiet. At first, the longer we sat, the more frightened I got. I used my peripheral vision to

keep an eye on Michelle, whose head was slowly turning, like radar. Every few seconds her left ear twitched.
I read once that a dog's hearing is sixteen times better
than a human's at certain frequencies. I wondered what
she was hearing. A couple times her hackles started to
go up, then quieted down.

After a while, I began to relax. The blood stopped
pounding in my ears. As my nerves calmed, I started to
hear better—the wind, the rustle of leaves, an occasional
chattering of a small animal somewhere. Then Michelle
put her head on my knee, gave a heavy sigh and lay
down. Only then did I fully relax.

Frank broke our silence: "Well, it'll make one helluva
story."

"Tell you the truth," I said, "if you tried to tell me a
story like this, I'd say you were full of it."

"We can prove it," said Frank.

"Right, we'll bag some of that smell and bring it
back." It wasn't until I said that that I realized how
strong that cat had smelled, a distinct odor directly
linked to my fear, and an odor that reminded me of the
big cat house at the Bronx Zoo.

"We'll bag some of that saliva she spit at us, bring it
back, have it analyzed, and voila! Our proof," said
Frank. Though his tone was lighthearted, the look on his
face was somber. He looked determined to stay
grounded, to prove this was not a dream.

"What's our next move?" he asked.

"I restart Michelle using the sweatband." I climbed
down from the rock and Michelle was right with me as
I hit the ground. She stuck her nose in the plastic bag
as I was fumbling to get it off my belt. Then she started
herself even before I said, "Go find." She took us back

toward the spot where she had turned off to follow the lion. I was enormously relieved when she continued on the original trail and away from the clearing. Now I was sure she was back on the kid's trail. At that moment, I felt like there was no better working dog in the world.

The boy had increased his lead on us, but after what we had been through, that was no big deal. We charged right along.

The early enthusiasm wore off in half an hour, however. The fatigue and cold were taking a toll. Remembering the two Snickers bars I had jammed into my pocket, I was about to announce a snack break when we saw car lights in the woods up ahead. We had been heading south but had stopped paralleling the road near the cemetery and the field some time ago. This had to be a different road.

A thirty-foot section of grass separated the woods from the road, which was bordered by a flat-topped stone-and-cement wall. Michelle jumped onto the wall, sniffed around a bit, then hopped off on the roadside and strode down the middle of the road, sniffing occasionally. We scrambled over the wall after her. Within a couple minutes, she stopped, then turned to face us. As I approached her, Michelle wagged her little stub tail sheepishly, as if to say, "I lost him." My heart melted with love.

I turned to Frank and said, "He hitchhiked or someone met him here."

The Aftermath:

Don got away. He made good his escape and went right to the place where the authorities would look first— his home.

Several months later, after he had been returned to the correctional facility, I had the chance to interview the kid. He didn't know that I was one of the men looking for him that night, and he bragged about how he had locked the searchers in the barn.

"I heard them so close a few times that if they had let the dog go, they would have had me in a minute," he said. "They really blew it there."

Then he described the location where a nice old farmer had stopped to give him a ride—right after he crossed the road after climbing over the stone wall. And he never heard any screams in the night.

His story enhanced my respect and love for Michelle because every detail verified her accuracy and excellence during the search. Not only did she put her life on the line for me, but she was right on his trail the whole night.

Halloween will always have a special significance for me. *Michelle, you make my heart sing.*

Training Notes

Sassy and Doris

Without any warning, a thirty-five-year-old man goes completely blind, from 20/20 vision to no vision whatsoever, in the course of two days. The impact is devastating. The mental journey from denial to rage to depression is long and arduous, with no guarantee of a successful adaptation.

Some time later this newly blind person is paired with a Seeing Eye dog. And what is the attitude of his new four-legged partner? Well, for one thing, there is no pity here. Four-legs is not saying to two-legs, "You poor thing!" or "Why you?" His feelings are expressed in his working attitude: "OK, you're blind, that's why I'm here, so let's make the best of it. I'll be your eyes and protect you and give you love, and in return you'll give me what I need, love and care."

Now imagine the reverse: Sassy is a sweet, loving,

intelligent and somewhat spoiled Shih-tsu who lost her sight from Sudden Advanced Retinal Degeneration. Her vet called me for help. The dog needed to be taught to adapt, but the real problem was with Doris, Sassy's owner. Doris was devastated, and was drowning Sassy in pity and sadness.

When I arrived at Doris and Sassy's house, I was relieved to see that Sassy was mentally stable, sweet and receptive to training. Doris, on the other hand, quickly became teary-eyed. Doris was clearly my first order of business.

"One of the most important, if not *the* most important thing I can share with people about dog training is the 'inadvertent rewarding of unwanted behavior,' " I told her. Doris's eyebrows went up. "Especially in the case of rewarding a fear response."

Now Doris was clearly interested, if confused. "A fear response?"

"Let's say you're walking down the street with your dog and a truck backfires. The dog hits the end of the leash shaking with fear. Most people will reward the dog for the fear response by soothing, petting, kissing and holding. This is the worst thing to do because they are literally teaching the dog to be fearful by praising the fear response. A better way to handle it is for the owner to respond to the sudden noise in a light-hearted tone with, 'Wow, did you hear that? Let's check that out.' The message is 'no big deal—get over it.'

"This applies to Sassy's blindness," I said, looking Doris in the eye. "When did pity ever help anyone? If pity does anything, it weakens. But Sassy is clearly ready to adapt and make the best of her condition.

When you and I get through with her, 99 percent of the people you meet won't even know she's blind unless you tell them."

"You're right, let's move forward," said Doris, surprising me with her sudden turnaround from grief.

"Then let's start with you first," I said. "I want you to make a noise by wearing something that jingles, like a bracelet or a cat bell. This will make it easy for Sassy to know where you are, to know your movement through the apartment, and it will improve her radar systems."

"Radar systems?" Again Doris's eyebrows went up.

"Yep, it isn't just her hearing that improves, it's everything—her sense of smell, her sensitivity to air pressure, temperature and air currents. She will become very aware of all the subtle environmental changes from room to room. Our immediate job is to keep Sassy mentally secure. If she's secure and feels safe enough, she'll keep exploring and adapting. But if she gets scared, she'll withdraw."

"Okay," said Doris, "how do we make her feel safe?"

I told her to get a pad and take notes, which she did. She sat down, pen in hand, and gave me a penetrating look.

"At the top of the page," I said, "write 'No Pity.' " She laughed and did so. Then I continued, "Get some carpet runners to use as pathways through the house. Each room will have a 'safe zone,' which will help Sassy reorient herself throughout the apartment. Her bed will be the safe zone in the living room, her pee-pad on one side of the kitchen, her food and water bowl on the other side of the kitchen, and another pee-pad and bed in the bedroom. Reaching any one of these safe zones will let her know exactly where she is and keep her oriented.

"Now for scents," I said. "I want you to get three distinct scents—one for the carpet runners, one for the safe zones, one for obstacles." That evening, Doris called to tell me that she had put a drop of vanilla extract every five feet or so on the runners. Then she put a drop of some strawberry essence at her beds and bowls and pee-pads. Finally, she put a tiny smear of Ben-Gay on all obstacles.

"Sassy's traveling around the house for the fun of it!" said Doris. "She's exploring and enjoying it."

"Great, now we'll finish by teaching her 'Easy,' which alerts her to slow down because of obstacles like wall corners and table legs. Also, 'Wait,' 'Come,' 'Left,' 'Right,' 'Let's go,' and 'Up and step' for going up and down steps and curbs."

Within two weeks we were in building hallways teaching Sassy turns and stops. Riding the elevator down, a family of four got on and the two children played with Sassy the entire ride down. When we got off the elevator, I mentioned that Sassy was blind. The look on their faces was worth a photo!

Before I left that day, Doris told me Sassy had taught her an important life lesson about "making the best of it." "But Sassy couldn't teach me if it weren't for you, Tom," she said. "I'll never forget what you did for us."

"My pleasure," I said. And it was.

3
A Dark, Dark Search

*The business phone rang a little past midnight, ech-*oing down the hall and into our bedroom. I heard it through layers of sleep, but I made no move to answer.

Then the home phone, on the nightstand by my pillow, trilled insistently. Someone wanted to reach me. Now. This call I took. Jaye, my wife, turned on her side to face me as I spoke, her eyes questioning.

"Tom, we need your dog right now." The caller was Mo, a fellow graduate of my police academy class. He lived about fifteen minutes away.

"I'll be right over," I said. "What's up?" The hour of his call and the anxiety in his voice prompted me to sit up as we spoke, the urge to sleep gone.

"One of my neighbors is missing. He went for a walk at noon this afternoon and hasn't returned. We need your dog right now."

At first I felt insulted by his lack of social grace. I had the urge to wake my dog, saying, "Michelle, wake up. Here are the car keys. They need you in Wesley Hills. Let me know how it works out."

But I shook off the mild insult. He wasn't asking for me, though Michelle went nowhere without her trainer. But then, I knew what he knew: I cannot smell what my dog smells. I, after all, am only human. My dog is the one who can follow the scent of the missing person. Michelle's ability to search and rescue may make a life-or-death difference on this cold November night.

As I headed toward the bathroom, a dark shadow followed me. Her big beautiful dark eyes smiled up as her stub tail wagged eagerly. How did she know?

Rushing to dress and gather supplies, I paused. Crawling out from under warm bedcovers in the middle of the night can skew your thinking on clothing needs. I stepped onto the bedroom deck to check the temperature and the humidity, a move that convinced me to pack extra clothing just in case.

From her cocoon under the covers, Jaye reminded me to pack some energy food and water. Water for Michelle. Searching dogs have to be kept well hydrated since constant search sniffing causes the olfactory glands to dry out, affecting the dog's ability to scent. This would be critical on a night like this when air currents might cause scent to pool or flow or drift.

Within ten minutes, I was ready. Even so, I forced myself through one final review of everything I had packed. I have always had to resist the temptation to dash off after I get "the call," but experience has taught me that if I'm not properly prepared, Michelle and I won't be at our best.

The November air was brisk, cold but not bitter. Still, it was not a great night for a walk. The sky was dark and impenetrable with no moon, no stars. The air was dank and heavy without even an interesting breeze to aid Michelle. That didn't bother her. She leaped enthusiastically into the car. That's my Michelle: she's happiest when she's working.

We had a ten-minute drive to the place last seen. As I drove into the night, determined to set aside my apprehension over weather conditions, I reviewed the information from Mo. The missing person was a thirty-nine-year-old male, married and the father of two, who had been knocked unconscious in a car accident five days earlier. He had remained unconscious for an hour and a half and had suffered headaches since. At noon he told his wife he was going for a short walk. Twelve hours later he had not returned.

That brief profile told me it was highly unlikely he was on a drunken binge, out with a girlfriend or had abandoned his wife and children. The accident worried me. I had an image of him lying on the side of a road or a path, having lost consciousness again.

As I drove, my palms turned sweaty and my stomach felt faintly queasy. These are my usual symptoms when I launch an SAR, especially when, as in this case, Michelle and I are the only K-9 unit. Everything depends on us. Our ability to locate the victim may make the difference between life and death. Time becomes infinitely precious as cool temperatures can cause hypothermia, quickly stealing a life. We have to maximize every moment.

In a perfect world, the K-9 SAR unit would be called first so that the dogs can work the area when it is least contaminated by other people's scents. The reality of a search for a missing person is quite different, however.

What usually happens is that the family calls friends first. When no one reports knowing where the missing person is, the family launches a ground search, enlisting the aid of friends and neighbors. When that doesn't work, the police are called. Soon the situation escalates into a full-blown search with a search command center crowded with trailers, emergency vehicles, ambulances, police cars, etc.

This changes the search area: with countless people trampling the site, it is now very contaminated. Worse yet, most emergency vehicles leave their engines running, generating a cloud of gas and fumes. Nothing does more to damage a working dog's ability to air scent than gasoline fumes. All these factors are why I try to park a good hundred yards away from any search site. On this night, I wasn't sure what to expect. Mo had told me he was involved as a neighbor, not as a cop, and that the police had not yet been called. I was hopeful.

By the time I parked, I was very nervous, which is normal for me. This is not to be confused with excitement over some sort of macho adventure. Quite the opposite. The possibility of saving a life, of being a hero, evaporates under the harsh reality of what lies ahead. At this stage, I am keenly aware that not all searches are successful, not all lives are saved.

I know, too, that I am about to face many people who have been looking unsuccessfully for a long time. They are frustrated, scared and worried—and they are looking to me for the quick find. Michelle and I are their only hope. If my dog can't find the victim . . . At this stage, I refuse to consider that option.

Instead, I concentrate on my dog. As we close in on the site, what is she thinking? Is she nervous like me? How does she interpret what is happening? I look over at her in the back of my Suburban. She is sitting up straight, staring intently out the window as if she needs to pick up visual details.

I know dogs. I train dogs for a living. I have read a great deal about dogs and their behavior. But I *live* with Michelle, as closely as with any family member. And I have spent a great deal of time observing her. I pick up on minute changes in her body language.

What I see right now is not apprehension but a state of "search alert." She must feel my nervous energy and I know she is familiar with the signs: my SAR vest and her water canteen.

As if to buoy my spirits, I remember another search and our trip home afterward. We were in the Pocono Mountains, where a fourteen-year-old boy was lost in a blizzard. We worked all night successfully. Thanks to Michelle's sending a search party in the right direction, the boy was returned to his joyous parents. I put Michelle in the Suburban and started our two-and-a-half-hour trip home.

The elation of the find soon wore off as the furious blizzard launched a sneak attack through crevices in the car, leaving my feet, wrists and hair damp and icy cold. Michelle, who had been so caked with snow and ice that a fellow searcher thought she was a white dog, had been dried off, given the command to "load up" into the car and was now curled into a warm donut, snoring loudly. Very loudly. Some partner, I thought as I forced myself to concentrate on the road. Listening to her snore while I struggled with terrible driving conditions, fatigue and the cold made me jealous enough to wake her up several times just to see her squinty-eyed look of love.

That memory of waking Michelle ended abruptly when I saw many people walking through the streets several blocks from the victim's house. When I pulled up to the house, it was surrounded by no fewer than 150 people.

I tensed, knowing I was about to face the parents, the wife and the children of the missing man. Knowing they are terrified and so am I. As I arrived, I could hear people saying, "Here's the dog. Thank God the dog is here." Leaving Michelle in the car, I went in search of Mo.

Inside the house was another mob scene, another 150-plus people. A low level of panic was apparent. Mo spotted me immediately. Others demanded to know why I left Michelle in the car, why hadn't I started searching? Ignoring them, understanding their anxiety, I asked Mo if we could speak privately. We found a bathroom and closed the door.

I explained to Mo that I needed a sense of the victim's state of mind. Was he getting along with his spouse? Was work going well? Did he have financial difficulties? Mo said that as far as he knew the victim had been experiencing nothing more than the normal hassles of daily life.

Next I spoke with the wife, listening and watching, alert to vibrations from her. She joined me along with her children, a boy and a girl about eight and ten years old. The fear on her face, the hope in her eyes when she saw me, made my heart feel heavy with responsibility.

Though I could see she was overwhelmed by the inexplicable situation, I received no unexpected vibes. Her state of mind was obvious: she loved her husband, she was very frightened, and she had told me everything she knew.

In a traditional woodland or forest search, I tell Michelle to "go find" any human being. That is because many searches are in remote areas with so few people around that the only one we are likely to come upon is the victim. This search, however, was in a neighborhood—an area packed with people, all of them strangers to Michelle.

This type of search is more challenging. It requires a clean scent article. Such an article can be tough to find. In this case, the victim's hat may have been handled by his son. His pillowcase and bedclothes had been lain upon by the wife and children and, by now, probably sat upon by neighbors.

I explained this to the victim's wife. She took me to a closet and pointed to a prayer shawl in a closed plastic bag. She assured me that no one except her husband touched the bag or the shawl. With a calculated casualness, I asked who had hung it in the closet after use. She insisted that she never touched it—her husband always put it back in the closet himself. Perfect.

Time to start. While talking to Mo and the family, I had been preparing to start Michelle working. Searching is more than a game to her: it is her *favorite* game. The key word in my SAR commands is *work*. The essential emotion is enthusiasm. I deliberately intensify both in my voice and my demeanor as we begin.

"Are you ready to *work*?" I ask Michelle, sounding happy in spite of our grim mission. Then, heightening the level of enthusiasm in my voice I repeat the key word: "We're going to *work*! Do you want to *work*?"

Her answer is obvious.

During most searches, Michelle works off-leash, ranging as far as a quarter mile away but always returning to confirm the general direction I want us to take. If she returns and picks up a stick, she is giving me an important signal: "I found the victim." When this happens, my *immediate* response is critical to our success as an SAR team. Her reward for a find must be a great deal of praise and stick play—tug-of-war and throwing the stick.

However, when she first brings the stick—before the reward is given—I say, "Show me." This is the "refind" command. She may have found the victim but I do not yet know where the person is. Remember, they could be lying unconscious, hidden under a log, two hundred yards away. "Show me" instructs Michelle to take me to the victim. *Then* we play. Even if the victim is "down" and in critical need of aid, I must take the time to praise my dog profusely before tending to the injured person. It takes only thirty seconds and it *has* to happen.

It isn't always easy either. I have had firemen react with astonishment when I ignore a victim while praising my dog and throwing a stick. I explain that if it were not for Michelle, the victim would not have been found. These thirty seconds of praise, this tugged and tossed stick, are all our heroine needs and wants for her efforts.

This search, however, would have to be conducted differently. Because it would be in a suburban neighborhood with car traffic, to which Michelle is oblivious when working, she would have to work on-leash. The harder she pulls on the leash, the closer she is to a find. In order to stay tuned to this alert from her, I use a harness instead of a collar.

All along, I had been thinking over where to start

Michelle amidst all the people and confusion. Incredibly, when I got back to the car, which was parked in the driveway of the house, there were twenty people tapping on the windows and looking at her. Michelle didn't know what to make of it.

Her natural instinct had prevailed and she was growling softly to protect the car, lips slightly raised. Being a Doberman, she's naturally "area-protective," but she has learned to distinguish the need for protection from everyday situations such as riding with our children's car pool. She never shows any protective aggression during these times, nor has she ever shown aggression from the car during a search, but then she had never been in a car surrounded by people tapping on the windows.

The moment we made eye contact, her face relaxed. But I was agitated by the scene because she had been made uncomfortable. It saddened me that this regal, loving dog probably felt gawked at like a caged animal in a zoo. She must be a little confused by the situation, which I found frustrating, because this was when I wanted her to focus on *finding* someone not *protecting* our car from someone.

I got her out of there as fast as I could and immediately redirected her focus and energy into working. She responded instantly. Together, we made our way through the throng back into the house. Michelle needed a taste of the victim's home. I knew that in spite of all the outsiders standing around, she would sense that he was a primary resident. To reinforce that, I focused on leading her to the master bedroom, his side of the bed, his closet and the chair he used at the kitchen table.

Finally, I gathered the wife and children with me by the closet that contained the prayer shawl for this reason:

with the possibility of more than one person's smell being found on a scent article, it helps to have all those
who may have touched the article present. I knew that
when Michelle smelled the article and picked up the
scent of three people other than the victim, she would
focus on the odor of the person *not* present. So with the
three key family members beside me, I pulled the bag
with the prayer shawl from the closet, opened it and said,
"Go find."

Michelle stuck her head into the bag and breathed
deeply. Boy, was she psyched! She turned, touched her
nose to the wife, who let out a slight gasp, grazed her
nose past the children—and headed toward the master
bedroom. Halfway there, she stopped, turned and started
toward the kitchen, stopped, started heading somewhere
else, then stopped one last time before heading out the
front door. Once outside, she made a right turn down
the side street toward a main thoroughfare. A perfectly
clear start.

She started for the bedroom after scenting the father's
presence most strongly in that location and used that as
a reaffirmation that he was her target. She was smart
enough to know he wasn't in the house, which is why
she turned around to follow his scent outside.

You cannot hide scent signposts from an air-scenting
dog like Michelle. That also explains why puppies can
act like distracted idiots on your front lawn—they are
being bombarded by stimuli. They are aware of the
squirrel that urinated on a blade of grass yesterday, the
bird that tried to catch a worm, the path of the ball
thrown by the little boy from next door. But the difference between a pup and an SAR dog is that the latter
has learned how to focus on the most critical scent.

This is one goal you work for when training an SAR dog. I remember my daughter's frustration at a children's dog obedience contest when she was six years old. The showring grass was littered with scraps of liver left by previous contestants. Tara was in the ring with Cheetah Ann, our previous dog. In spite of the fact that both the puppy and the child knew what to do, little Cheetah Ann's performance was marred by her constantly sniffing out the previously thrown pieces of liver. Tara left the ring in tears while Cheetah Ann grazed for more liver.

Now, within seconds I was being dragged down the street by Michelle while someone in the crowd shouted, "Don't go there, we looked in that direction already." I paid no attention. Actually, at the moment, I was euphoric. Michelle was working and pulling with such enthusiasm than I anticipated a quick find. All I could imagine, based on my experience searching with Michelle, was that the victim lay unconscious very close by.

As she pulled me forward, I noticed the temperature had dropped significantly. It had to be freezing, if not colder. Not a good night to be lying unconscious under a starless black sky. When Michelle got to the corner, she turned right without hesitating, pulling me with her onto a much busier road. She kept going . . . and going . . . and going. Thirty minutes into this dead heat straight ahead, she lost her "pull." The confidence and assurance of her gait had vanished.

Working her into the wind, I restarted her at the point where I felt she lost the trail. We worked through some ditches and past several streams and culverts, which bordered a school campus. No luck. Then suddenly she

showed interest at an intersection and started us down
that street with a purposeful pull.

I didn't like it. This was a very quiet, very long, very
dark street. I could see the shadows of large trees, faint
outlines of houses set far back from the road. No sounds
or lights even came from the massive black shadows.
Then the road curved left to disappear into absolute
blackness. I saw no sign of human life in this yawning
black hole. Still Michelle pulled. In fact, she was happy
and enthusiastic, pulling me with great determination
down the center of that dark road.

I am rarely spooked but this search had the hairs on
the back of my neck standing straight up. And I was
jumpy. Michelle felt my anxiety. Or did she feel her
own? Although working hard, she, too, seemed skittish
and was looking about warily. Now the long left curve
swung right, leading into another black hole. We had
been going for over an hour and a half. I was aware of
the cold and a touch of fatigue.

Again, Michelle's enthusiasm started to wane. I was
about to stop us both for a brief rest when I saw a light
in the far distance. It looked like a streetlamp at an intersection. Michelle, meanwhile, had begun to drift
about as if she had lost the scent. I decided we should
head to the intersection to see if she might pick up the
scent along the way. If she didn't, then my plan was to
let her pick the direction from the intersection. If she
gave no definite sign, I would retrace our steps back to
a point where I knew she had "had scent."

The light was farther away than it appeared—fifteen
minutes away. Once there Michelle gave no sign. So I
swung my arm to indicate that we should go back and

started walking. She loped in front of me as if she was out for a stroll in a meadow.

"Concentrate, Michelle," I said. I was frustrated, worried and tired. Worried because the temperature was now at a hazardous level. If the victim was down, he was probably hypothermic and close to death. Frustration and anger were the result of my initial high hopes for a quick find. However, the last thing I ever want to do is communicate negatively with my dog. Guess what I had just done.

I had given the word *concentrate* a caustic edge and I regretted that. Michelle's flickering ears told me she had registered my comment and felt chastised. To make up for my harsh words, I spoke again—this time with dedicated encouragement. I made myself work harder at the *game*.

Now Michelle turned around. She smiled at me and wagged her stub tail as if to say, "I'm trying, Dad, I'm trying." My heart felt a little lighter at the sight. I love to see her stub tail wag. How could I have doubted her for a moment? She is so loyal and hard-working and determined to do the right thing.

Fifteen minutes later, Michelle changed gears. We had been backtracking through that surreal dark tunnel of a road. Fog was rolling in now, making it even more difficult to see. Then it happened: Michelle gave a muffled yelp and made a sharp left turn onto someone's lawn. Her nose reached up and I knew she was air scenting.

That signal left me no choice but to follow her through backyards. This is my least favorite pastime. There is a real possibility of being reported to the police as a prowler, being chased by homeowners who may possess firearms, or being assaulted by irate home-protecting dogs. Foreign backyards do not make me comfortable. On this night it was an endless number of yards and fences with Michelle's nose pointed in one direction: north.

I was excited by Michelle's burst of enthusiasm and completely forgot my fatigue and concern over the cold. Minutes later we came to another road that curved into a small wooded park. Michelle was air scenting and wanted to cut into the park straight through a heavy ground cover of thornbushes and briars. I wasn't surprised.

I spotted a path that led in the direction Michelle wanted to go, so I directed her to it. As a puppy, to my chagrin, she used to dive right into the bushes. But a major difference in Michelle since then has been her willingness to accept redirection, to be patient and work with me to find the best, easiest route to get where she knows we need to go.

Once on the path, all I had to do was keep up. She was pulling hard. We ran by several neighbors who had already been searching the park. Suddenly, as the road ended and the path into the woods began, someone yelled, "Be careful, it's slippery"—just as my feet hit the ice. I must have been a funny sight. I really didn't want to go sprawling in front of all these people so I made strenuous efforts to keep my balance. But try as I might, arms and legs flailing in twenty different directions, I was airborne, then landing hard and sliding a good fifteen feet on the ice. I yelled, "Wait," to Michelle, who was pulling me relentlessly across the ice.

I called her back to me. She came, waiting impatiently while I unhooked her leash with the words, "Go find him now."

And as I spoke those words, a sense of foreboding swept over me so strong that I shivered. After the search, I reflected on that rush of coldness: I wasn't psychic. Michelle had signaled me with something barely perceptible in her manner, but a change that I could intuit. That shows you how closely an SAR trainer and his dog are tuned. Michelle and I have not come upon death often, but when it is out there, we both know before we see.

I scrambled to my feet, forgetting my pride, forgetting my happiness that we were close to a find. All I felt was sadness—and fear. Michelle left, then returned. She picked up a stick halfheartedly and dropped it in front of me.

"Show me," I said, running after her as she broke into a trot. We passed other searchers as we ran. Michelle's trot became a run. The path turned right but she ran straight ahead into the woods and across a little stream to stop about a hundred feet from the water. As I pushed through the brush to follow her, I thought of the victim's wife and children and the fear in their faces.

"He'll be okay," I said out loud, but I felt like I was about to cry.

"He'll be—" I started again and stopped. I couldn't believe what I was seeing. Twenty feet ahead of me was the victim, lying on the ground and partially obscured by a tree. On one side of the tree I could see his legs, on the other his head. Only the head looked like a bubble. A fuzzy bubble.

I checked the legs—they appeared normal. I approached slowly, waiting for the weird bubble of a head to make sense. Even when I stood directly over him, it took me several seconds to understand what I was looking at. His head was encased in a plastic bag, which was tied so that it closed sloppily around his neck. I knelt to remove the bag. The eyes were lifeless. Those seconds of staring into that dead face froze themselves in my mind. Then I noticed his arm was contorted unnaturally. And from the corner of my eye, I saw Michelle sniffing with interest around the scene.

But there was no time to mourn, not even to sigh with despair. The running man and his dog had been followed. The word was out: "He's here. The dog found him. Over here!"

As I was rewarding Michelle, people swarmed over the site, pushing to see. I tried to keep them back, shouting that this was a crime scene that had to be preserved.

"Call the EMTs," I cried, hoping against hope that they might revive him. But the EMTs refused to use a defibrillator with the body lying partially in snow and ice. I helped to carry the body out, then returned to the scene with Mo to do what we could to preserve the already trampled area until the police could arrive.

I don't even remember the ride home. I know I praised Michelle a lot but I felt numb. When I got home, sometime between 4 and 5 A.M., I woke Jaye and told her the whole story, my attempt at a critical-incident stress debriefing. It didn't work. Neither of us could sleep after that. Later that morning, Jaye had me recount the entire story again in hopes a retelling would relieve my stress.

In reliving the search, one thing became very clear to me—the victim may have been picked up by a car. Why do I think that? The victim's body was found five minutes from his house. You came out his front door, made a left turn, then another left and a right into the woods, *but that is not the path he took to the woods that day*. Instead he made a right out of his house, then another right. How can I be so certain? Michelle told me.

The basic axiom of K-9 SAR is *Trust your dog*, and Michelle has taught me to believe that. This situation was similar to the one when she and I worked the search for the teenager, Don, who escaped from the juvenile detention center. Michelle had lost the scent. But, when the boy was found and I questioned him, he bragged about fooling us. He fooled us because he hitched a ride—at the exact spot where Michelle had lost the scent. That's why I believe our victim on this dark search also got into a car.

This is also why I go out of my way to talk to people after they are found. I need to know where they went and why because it gives me added insight on why my dog does what she does. Most errors made during a search are made by the dog handler, not the dog. My dog knows what has happened. I just have to read her better. I constantly marvel at Michelle. Her interest, her effort, her ability level is so high. I cannot let her down by misinterpreting her signals.

Suicide, murder or accident, none of that changes my grim memory of this dark search and the feeling of possibly giving false hope to the wife and children whose lives were shattered by the find. Silly to think that way but sometimes I can't help it.

Did Michelle and I offer false hope to the wife and children? No. We gave them their only hope. And that is why Michelle and I will meet that challenge again and again.

Training Notes

Smokey and Bandit

Whenever I hear a dog is misbehaving and "he does it for no reason at all," I know that's wrong. *There is always a reason.*

Take Shatsi, for example. His owner could not figure out why Shatsi kept digging at the baseboard of the wall of the living room. New Sheetrock was now needed for the second time.

"She has everything a dog could want and still she does this to my walls," said the flummoxed owner, "and for no reason at all."

"Well," I said, "Shatsi could be neurotic or have a neurological problem or just be bored—but in this case? Call an exterminator."

The owner's face went blank.

"Mice," I said. "I've seen wall digging before and I suggest you check for rodents before we work with the dog." I was right and it took only a session or two to redirect Shatsi away from the walls.

Another case shows why dog training requires you to be a darn good sleuth. Smokey and Bandit were one of my toughest cases to crack.

I was called because Smokey was behaving very aberrantly. He was four years old, a charming miniature schnauzer. Well trained, he would get his leash when told, food bowl, certain toys, Dad's slippers, and he would hit the bells hanging on the back door when he wanted to go out. He was intelligent, wanted to please and was very communicative in his responses to me and his owners. I wasn't sure what the problem was.

"He's acting different . . . depressed maybe . . . scared . . . doing things he never did before like moving things, barking for no reason. We've come home to find him under the coffee table cowering, and he's urinated in the house twice! He never does that!"

I wondered if it was some anxiety syndrome but asked the owners to get a complete medical checkup done on the dog first. Two weeks later, after the dog was found to have no health problems, I visited again. And again Smokey was responsive and engaging, his eyes sparkling with intelligence and understanding. Still, his owners were concerned.

"The two biggest problems," said his owner, "is his barking when we're not home, and when we are home, he acts as if he's afraid of us."

"Okay," I said, "let's sit down somewhere. I have a lot of questions."

They showed me into their kitchen, a large airy room with another resident of the house: "Hello, welcome, my name is Bandit, me casa your casa." An African Gray parrot greeted me, sounding just like one of the owners.

"Neat bird," I said and sat down to write up about four hundred questions, none of which solved the problem. "Let me think on this."

During my forty-minute drive home, I mulled over the perplexing situation with Smokey. I couldn't figure it out but I never give up. Then I remembered something I read once about the intelligence of animals— that intelligence was not a factor of brain size but of the weight of the brain in relation to the weight of the body. Birds have hollow bones and feathers, making their brains very heavy in proportion to their bodies. The article also stated that some birds, African Grays among them, are extremely smart, even smarter than dogs.

I couldn't wait to get home—I called from the car. "I know this sounds a little weird," I said to Smokey's owners, "but I would like you to get a noise-activated tape recorder and leave it on the kitchen table while you are gone. Listen to it when you get home and call me."

At three the next day I had an excited client on my tape recorder. "Tom! When we got home today, Smokey was cowering under the coffee table. Right away we remembered the tape recorder so we listened.

"You were right! Bandit was imitating the doorbell, causing Smokey to charge the door and bark. He must have done it at least ten times. No wonder the neighbors are complaining. Then he yells at Smokey, sounding just like us. He calls him 'a bad boy' and curses at him just like we do. But we always do it in a kidding way. Bandit sounds so mean—but he sounds just like our voices. I hate that bird!"

Bandit had been playing Smokey like a violin. And so he was relegated to another section of the house, behind a closed door, while the owners were gone. Smokey needed a light treatment for separation anxiety and then he was his old self.

And me? They call me "Detective Tom." Remember: there is always a reason.

Training Notes

Pecking Order: An Owner's Dilemma

Dogs are pack animals, social beings who enjoy the company of others. This explains why many dogs will not touch their food when left alone but will wait to eat in the company of their owners. Not only is eating a social activity for dogs but they eat according to pecking order. In a litter of puppies, that pecking order is established by age fourteen weeks.

This pecking order is critically important to dogs and was established by their ancestors. A wolf pack had to hunt cooperatively in order to stay alive, which would be impossible if they were fighting among themselves. And so order was established and insubordination squashed. Just as hierarchy worked for the Roman legions and for the marines, so it has worked for the dog.

Michelle lives in a pack of seven: me, Jaye, Tara,

Kerry, Brett, Michelle and Tri. Michelle ranks number six and Tri is number seven. It has to be this way, as in the human-dog pack harmony can't exist unless the dog is behind the last human being in this order. It is up to the owner to ensure this. However, the pecking order of the dogs is up to the dogs—human pack members have no say over who is "top dog." This is one of the few times that dogs should dictate and owners take direction.

It was difficult explaining this to my client Louellen. At her vet's urging, she had called me because her new puppy, Rocky, had been in a serious fight with her other dog, Peanut. Serious enough to send Peanut to the vet with two bites that drew blood.

When I arrived at Louellen's home, I found Peanut to be more of a princess than a peanut. A six-year-old toy poodle, she had been carried, pampered and spoiled to the extent that I told her owner, "When I'm reincarnated, I want to come back as your dog."

The reason for the new dog was that Louellen had been very busy with her work and wanted Peanut to have a playmate when she couldn't be there. And so she had arrived home one day with another toy poodle, fifteen-week-old Rocky.

Ideally, when introducing a new dog into a household that already holds a dog, the doggy introduction should take place outside the home, off the property and on neutral ground. Dogs are hardwired for territorial aggression and will defend their pack and their territory from any intruders. Thus the best approach is for the dogs to meet elsewhere and then come back to the house together. But that's not what Louellen had done.

When I met Rocky, he was eight months old. A white poodle to match Peanut, he was taller, lanky and had attitude. Not a bad attitude, he just had a presence to him. He was confident, outgoing, curious, engaging, charming, sensitive and smart. I liked him.

Eight months in dog life meant that he was on the cusp of exiting junior high, a punk age, and heading for young adulthood. He showed all the promise of being a quality dog, a "keeper"—a dog I would keep for myself. A characteristic I really liked about Rocky was that he was a leader and a levelheaded dog, not one given to excessive dominance behavior.

Peanut, in spite of being spoiled, was a sweet, smart dog herself. She just wasn't thrilled with a new upstart in her home, her territory, and was treating him accordingly.

The problem was that Rocky had reached an age when he was not going to be pushed around anymore. Now, some dogs will play second fiddle to smaller dogs. I knew an Italian greyhound named Harold who couldn't have weighed six pounds, yet ruled a roost of three other dogs, including a 180-pound mastiff named Brutus. When Harold told Brutus to scram, it was hard not to laugh as that huge mastiff would slip and slide in his haste to obey.

But when Peanut pushed, Rocky pushed back. He knew he was right to be dominant. Had he come into the home of a larger, more dominant dog, he wouldn't have fought the battle because he was reasonable and knew his limitations. That's not true of all dogs. I knew a little Yorkie once who inadvertently committed suicide by attacking a Great Dane. Rocky was smart enough to know what was rightfully his.

Training those two dogs was easy. Both were smart and quick to respond. They disproved that old saying, "you can't teach old dogs new tricks," which is false anyway. It's much easier to teach older dogs new tricks—like teaching a twenty-year-old how to drive a car as opposed to a five-year-old. By the end of three lessons, both dogs were answering my commands.

The problem was Louellen. I had to get her to understand and support the new pecking order.

"How can I do that!" she choked the first time I laid out what she had to do to keep the peace. "Peanut's been my constant companion for six years, I can't treat Rocky better than her. I won't do it!"

"Louellen," I coaxed, "you don't have to treat Rocky better, *just first.* Look, if you had four dogs and came home with presents for all four but shoved the alpha dog away and gave the first present to the lowest-ranking dog, guess what? The other dogs would beat him up and take the present. By not supporting the pecking order, you are making it worse for the dog you're trying to help."

"So what am I supposed to do?" Louellen was quite doubtful. This was a serious dilemma for her.

"Help Peanut by always greeting Rocky first, picking him up first, feeding him first, putting him on the bed first, giving him treats first, presents first, leash first and loving him first. Not loving him stronger or better—*just first.*

"Since Rocky is less needy than Peanut, once they're on the bed, you'll find you can spend more time snuggling Peanut—so long as Rocky is on that bed first. And don't be afraid to use the 'Enough' whistle."

I had taught Rocky and Peanut to immediately cease any aggressive behavior toward each other at the sound of this whistle, which Louellen wore on a chain around her neck, prompting me to call her Coach.

Months later, she told me that she wouldn't have been able to stick to this new regimen without my constant support. But she hung in there and her dogs responded. Today they are inseparable siblings with Rocky as the older brother—*even though he's five years younger!*

4

*The Blizzard and the Unsung Hero—Our
Strangest Search*

The night was about to go from good to perfect. The
kids were tucked in, the weather forecast said snow was
on the way, and the Jacuzzi was filling. With luck the
snow would be falling just as Jaye and I got into the
water. Nothing like watching the snow through the sky
window when we've got water up to our chins, tucking
us in like a blanket. What more can one ask?

As usual, my wife was in first, telling me which can-
dles to light and which lights to turn off as she squeezed
her hands together tightly, a habit she has when she's
happy. After three kids and a bunch of years of marriage,
I'm astute enough to know that the happier my partner
is, the happier I'll be.

At last it was time. I had completed all Jaye's ambi-
ance requests and I was just taking my shirt off when
the phone rang. To this day I don't understand why I

answered instead of letting it ring. Under normal circumstances, I wouldn't have. I'm not that kind of guy. And
I know that had I already hopped into the hot tub, I
would not have gotten the message until the next morning—for sure.

After taking the call, I walked back to the Jacuzzi.
Jaye took one look at my face and knew the party was
over. "Oh my God, what?" she said.

"It's a search for a missing person."

"Don't go." Jaye's response was immediate and
strong. "Tom, don't go. You don't have to, you're a
volunteer. You've always gone when called but it's late,
it's snowing—and it's Christmas, for Pete's sake." (In
truth, this was only the fourth official call-out for me
and Michelle, now two years old, and the date was De-
cember 27 and it hadn't started to snow, yet.)

Still, she was absolutely right and I wouldn't have
gone except for one hitch.

"It's a fourteen-year-old kid missing since two-thirty
this afternoon and it's highly probable he's still alive."

Jaye's face changed. "Oh no, just Tara's age," she
said. "You have to go."

"I know."

Tara is our firstborn. Kerry and Brett are three and
five years younger. Not looking for a lost kid under these
circumstances was so unthinkable to either one of us that
Jaye was already out of the Jacuzzi and quizzing me on
the location of the search. Before I could answer, she
was listing the energy snacks she would put together for
us. Her ability to go from pause to fast forward never
fails to impress me. Especially when it's needed.

"It's in the mountains," I said.

"Oh no, it'll take you hours just to get there, Tom."

"I know." The reality of what I was about to do hit me. I must have sounded like I was about to cry because she stepped forward and wrapped her arms around me, holding me until she could feel me calm down a little. Jaye is very tuned to me, a true empath. Whenever I've misplaced my courage or fortitude or strength, she knows how to use our closeness to communicate just what I need.

Standing so close together, I let myself breathe her in until I felt my adrenaline kick in. She was practically naked as she hugged me and I could feel her body still hot from the tub. After a moment, she pulled back, looked up at me, and said exactly what I needed to hear: "I'll be waiting for you."

That's how that search got started. And, brother, it was one I was not up for. That's not usually the case— like the search when the call came in at ten on a lazy Sunday morning. The timing on that one was perfect. I had slept late, had a relaxed breakfast and was looking at doing some long-put-off chores when the call to help find a missing mental patient came in. Now that's the way I like it. I was delighted to know I'd be spending a beautiful day in the woods rather than cleaning the garage. Of course, I never do get it quite right. I left the house happily that day, telling Jaye I expected to make a find by midafternoon and be home for an early dinner. Boy, was I wrong. That missing person was never found.

On this night the victim was a fourteen-year-old named Chris. He had been hunting with his father, uncle and other friends when he somehow got separated from the group. Though they noted he had been missing since

2:30, they had searched for hours before calling for help.

As I got everything ready, we had one slight delay when I couldn't find Michelle's winter coat. Jaye wouldn't let me leave without it because of the snow and because we were heading into the Poconos. We did have our SAR vests, however. Michelle's vest is orange and always in a state of readiness—as is Michelle. There's nothing she'd rather do than go on a search. It's a comfort to know you have a partner who is always more than willing. I can wake her up in the middle of the night anytime, any place, and she is always raring to go. In fact, she's useless for the first few moments of the search. I have to wait while she runs around like crazy, taking the edge off her exuberance, and only then do I release her with a "Go find." I love it.

My vest and preparation is a little more complicated. Not only do I keep it as close as a fireman would, but I make sure it's properly stocked and updated and ready to go on a moment's notice. Finally, having gathered together her coat and our SAR vests, we were ready.

Hunched over to tie my boots, I felt Michelle's presence. I glanced up to see her staring at me with that big super smile of hers. How did she know what was happening? Easy.

The new sounds and movements, different from what had been happening earlier in our home, alerted her. She could sense the electricity between Jaye and me just as she could sense my excitement. I can't help it. Whenever I get a search call, my reactions are immediate and obvious. The mix of excitement and fear that runs through me is communicated directly to Michelle. Not to mention that the moment she spotted her coat and search vest she knew what was up and reacted instantly.

She had her nose next to my ear with her face gently touching mine as she whined softly. So there I was lacing up my boots with a Doberman whispering to me. I whisper back, ever so softly but very intensely, "Patience, Bell, and soon we'll go to work and have some fun." The zeal in my whisper and the word *work* hit home with Michelle. She recognizes both the emotion in my communication as well as the word *work*, which is a key signal between us and one I use to psyche her up before a search.

From this point on, she will wait for me as patiently as a well-trained search dog can given that she's ready to explode with excitement and anticipation. She'll shadow my every move and whine at me to hurry up.

Once we're in the car she relaxes. It's uncanny how she knows, but to Michelle being in the car is a sign that our search is a done deal: a search is about to take place and she is included. For Michelle, our drive time is down time, time to rest up before the adventure. During this stage, she reminds me of a martial arts expert meditating up to the moment before a contest.

The drive was fine for the first hour. Then snow started to fall, light and airy with flakes just teasing the windshield. When it didn't get any heavier after the first ten minutes, I was convinced we would have a dusting and I'd soon be out of it.

Suddenly the teasing stopped. The road disappeared. The world went white with frenzy, like an insane snow dance. Snowflakes were leaping, diving and twisting with such intensity that they appeared to be attacking the car. My windshield wipers went from a dead stop to full speed but only added to the surreal scene. It took intense concentration to focus on the road that lay somewhere behind all the insane movement of the snow. I switched my headlights from high to low beam and back again to help me focus and find the road. I found it difficult to avoid staring into the snow hitting the windshield. A quick glance out my side window revealed zero visibility, just a million more frenzied snowflakes. Within seconds after running into this wall of snow, the road surface changed from normal to several inches of slippery powder.

I was grateful to be in a four-wheel-drive Suburban. A regular car would have been absolutely impossible to manage under these conditions. And with each mile the conditions deteriorated. Route 84 became an obstacle course. Cars were stopped all over the place, some with their lights off.

I was taken aback when I approached a low-grade incline and found cars and trucks stuck along the highway in every imaginable position—facing traffic, broadside to traffic, doing slow 360s in an effort to get up the hill. Eighteen-wheelers were mired in snow, some jackknifed. I had never seen anything like this. The only things moving were four-wheel-drive vehicles. It was as if we were the only living creatures passing through a graveyard of recently deceased hulks. The hulks looked sullen and angry as I passed each one—and I was more than a little unnerved.

Conditions continued to worsen. The snow fell harder and it piled deeper and deeper on the roadway, which caused my car to slip more in spite of four-wheel drive. This had become more than a white-knuckle drive. It had gone beyond the call of duty and I was ready to quit. I decided to look for an exit so I could turn around and head home. Right then the highway ended, the road shoulder began and the entire universe was whited out.

I don't know how long I had been driving in this twilight zone when I was able to make out a sign that said "Sta Pol" with an arrow pointing to an off ramp. This gave me an idea as I skidded to a slow stop near the sign. First, I looked in the rearview mirror before I got out of the car. Nothing was moving behind me. I found a tree branch to brush the snow from the sign and confirm that it said "State Police." Five minutes later I was in an intersection with no idea which way it was to the police station. There were, however, the nearby lights of a twenty-four-hour convenience store.

When I told the proprietor my story, he invited me to bring my dog inside and said that we could have anything we wanted on the house. Meanwhile, he called the police for me.

Michelle found this interesting. She had never been in a store like this before and I wasn't telling her to "Go find." I, meanwhile, had some luck—even with all the road emergencies, there were two gendarmes in the station. My first question to them was, "Is the search for the boy still on or has he shown up?" This was in the days before I had a cell phone for each car. The question is pretty important as many SAR team members have arrived at search locations only to find the victim has been found or was never really missing.

But the search was still on. The officer I had reached told me the boy was still missing and the search was on full-bore in spite of blizzard conditions. It was, he said, "quite possible for the boy to still be alive but unlikely to make it through the night." So much for my thoughts of quitting.

The officer said he had managed to get back to the

station to get outfitted with snow chains for his police car, which was now ready, and he would be over in a few minutes to lead me to the search site. "You'll never find it yourself," he said. "Don't go anywhere, just sit tight until I get there."

I resisted making a sarcastic comment when he repeated himself, saying, "Don't go anywhere—we can use your help."

"Go anywhere?" I wanted to say. "I want to go into a fetal position and sleep." Talk about mixed emotions— searches generate the best and the worst. Make a find and you save a life. Don't make a find and maybe someone dies. At times the pressure is exhilarating and pumps me up, other times I'm a nervous wreck.

This was a nervous wreck moment. I was cold and wet from the walk through the snow to the store and I was exhausted, even nauseous, from the nerve-wracking drive. And the search hadn't even begun!

Michelle, meanwhile, was having a great time. The store manager felt she should be given high-energy food before starting her journey so he offered her whatever she looked at. By the time I put an end to the feast, she had consumed a Snickers, peanut brittle, a corn muffin, Lifesavers, several powdered donuts and a Hostess cupcake. She had powder all over her face, a blob of cream from the cupcake on her nose, and the biggest smile on her that I'd ever seen. I couldn't help but laugh as I told her, "Enough."

Her happiness was contagious. You don't need a blood pressure machine to document that what they say about dogs lowering blood pressure is true. Just one look at Michelle's happy, relaxed, trusting, loving and ridiculous cream-covered face and the tension drained right out of me. It started at my neck, spread down through my shoulders and continued down until the stress flowed through my feet and out my toes. That's what it felt like—melted and washed away.

I squatted to face Michelle. We have a routine we've shared since she was a pup. I call it our "Vulcan dog mind meld." Sounds weird but it works for us. I put my face next to hers, making light contact, and say, "V-d-m-m."

"V-d-m-m." We do it before and during both real and practice searches. It relaxes and psyches us both. As our faces touch, I can feel her energy. I can also feel the love and excitement she feels for the hunt we're about to start. It injects me with confidence, empowers us both *and we love it.*

Doing what we do, I understand why men hunt. I think it goes back to the beginning of time. I know that while I find hunting a living thing to be intensely exciting, hunting for a man is far more exciting than hunting a deer. In my experience, I've seen that dogs share that "hunt lust." Dogs on point vibrate with intense anticipation. Did you ever see a terrier chase down a rat? It's compelling. Michelle and I must have been doing our "V-d-m-m" for a good thirty seconds before the light from the arriving patrol car reflected off the store windows.

Time for the next stage, the one that would bring us closer to the actual hunt. The sheriff's deputy entered the store, stomping snow off his boots and, eyes closed, bellowing three enormous sneezes. This was not good.

All dogs are protectively territorial to some extent, some breeds much more than others. Dobermans rank very high on the list. That is basically what they are bred for. Given that, the best action that Jesse, the police officer coming at us in the store, could have taken was to look at my dog, make eye contact for a split second, and then proceed to say "hi" to both of us and engage me in conversation. An entrance of that type would have diffused much of Michelle's protective territorial instinct by conning her into thinking the police officer was a welcome arrival as opposed to an intruder.

Instead, he came at us like a snorting, stomping bull about to go on a rampage. When he finished with his explosive sneezing fit, he tried to rip his hat off but it got caught when he couldn't get the hood of his parka back far enough. That's when he slipped on the wet floor and went into a crazy, arms-flailing dance as he struggled to keep his balance. He didn't fall, but it wasn't until he regained his balance that he finally looked up to see Michelle. He froze, eyes wide.

Even though I found his entrance to be one of the funniest I've ever seen, Michelle was short on humor. The moment Officer Jesse stopped stomping, you could hear her low throaty growl. By the time he had composed himself, he was looking at a Doberman pinscher that had her lips curled back as far as they could go. He had to think he was looking at the bared teeth of a skull.

Michelle's hackles were up now and she approached the officer very slowly as she continued to growl in a way that was extremely menacing. This was an extreme reaction for Michelle. I had never seen her act so aggressively, but then I'd never seen a worse entrance. Of course, he was looking at a dog whose face was still covered in cream and powder. He told me later he thought she was "a foaming, rabid dog."

"Leave it," I said to Michelle in a sharp tone as I

approached the officer with my hand outstretched. "Tom Shelby, thanks for coming so fast to help me out. I don't think I could find my way back to the highway in this storm, never mind to the search site," I said as we shook hands.

"I don't think she likes me very much," he said, looking over my shoulder at Michelle.

"About as much as a grizzly with bad intentions crashing through that door," I said and laughed.

"Will she get over it or is this now a lifetime deal with her?" He smiled.

I liked Officer Jesse immediately. He had a broad, open face and a manner that made me feel I could rely on him. "I gave her the 'Don't kill' command so you're good for the moment," I said. "Just don't slip again."

"Great," he said with a wry smile, "ready to go?"

"Let's do it."

Jesse glanced at Michelle, still a little uncertain as he turned to leave. I gave her a quick hand signal that meant "Stay."

"I'll be right there, Officer," I said, then walked over to Bob, the store owner, to shake his hand. "Thanks for your help and hospitality—I know Michelle won't forget your generosity." (I thought, but refrained from saying— I hope she doesn't get the runs from the chocolate!)

"I hope you find the kid," he responded.

Under normal circumstances, nobody is more enthusiastic about searching than Michelle, but to my surprise she balked. She stopped at the open door and looked back at Bob. Maybe it was the snow and wind hitting her in the face that made Bob, his donuts and the warm store look good.

"Time to go to work, load up, please." At my goading,

she bounded out to the truck and jumped in as I opened the door.

The ride to the search site was very slippery. What should have taken five minutes took us a good fifteen. When we got there, the search command site reminded me of the movie *Apocalypse Now*—only here it was freezing, not sweltering.

Through a fog of swirling, blowing snow, I could barely make out the multicolored blinking lights of various types of emergency vehicles. "I'll be back in a few minutes," I told Michelle as I jumped out of the truck and headed for the command center.

It was a scene that seemed lit with psychedelic flares. Clouds of gasoline vapors combined with all the flashing lights to create an ethereal hue that looked to me like life on a different planet. I would have paused to relish the mesmerizing effect except for the wind howling in my ears and the snow stinging my face. I also felt the urgency of the full-court press I was about to encounter: we had to find that boy now! Conditions were already so dangerous for the searchers that we were once again reminded that we were on a strictly voluntary basis.

Stepping into the large RV that served as the command post was like stepping through a portal into another world. I was engulfed in warmth and bustle and not a little taken aback by the loud static-filled conversations coming from the radio, which was turned up full blast. Jesse waved to someone at the other end of the trailer and Nevil, the search coordinator, came right over to introduce himself.

"We've had two bloods out there for hours—nothing. Thanks for coming, you're the only other dog to show up."

I liked him immediately because I could tell he was a dog guy. He referred to the bloodhounds as "bloods," something only someone familiar with working noses is likely to say.

"Unless they go to the air, the bloods will have to be incredibly lucky to pick up a trail without a PLS," I said. Bloodhounds normally keep their noses to the ground following foot trails. They are not allowed to air scent, so without a clue to a victim's place last seen, an air scenter like Michelle is often more helpful.

"What have you got?" I said, looking for a summary of the situation.

"What have *you* got?" he asked.

It took me a minute, but then I responded, "A Dobe."

"Is she good?" Nevil looked me in the eye.

The proud daddy almost blurted out, "the best," but I restrained myself. "She'll work," I said, "if she picks him up, she'll tell me."

The next few minutes were spent poring over maps as Nevil pointed out the areas already covered by foot searchers and the bloods. Then he gave me a brief profile of the missing kid and the situation. He basically confirmed what I already knew: Chris had been hunting with family and friends and got separated from them in the early afternoon. The hunting party had searched for him for several hours before notifying the authorities. He was dressed warmly but not prepared for snow, not to mention spending the night in a howling blizzard.

I wanted more information about Chris as a person. I find thorough profiles to be helpful. Is the kid shy or bold? Dependent or independent? Does he show a lot of common sense for a fourteen-year-old or not?

I pride myself on asking good questions. I practice

with a game I like to play with friends and family. It goes like this: Think of someone we both know—or know of—and I will try to guess who it is. I get only one guess but I can ask as many questions as I want before making that guess. You must answer all my questions with a simple yes or no. The game is good because it teaches the art of questioning.

As I asked questions about Chris, I discovered one piece of news that I thought might be major—the kid had a rifle. Had anyone heard any shots? Did the family and friends looking for him earlier fire any shots of their own to see if they got a response? All I got for answers were blank looks from Nevil and everyone around him.

"I want to speak to the kid's father," I said.

He was two trailers away, warming up and resting with the rest of the hunting party and the boy's mother, who had arrived several hours earlier after learning of her son's absence. I questioned Chris's dad for a good fifteen minutes and learned many more specifics about his son's personality, state of mind, attire and the chronology of events. None of it was very encouraging, especially the fact that no one heard any gunshots.

So what did this mean? Could the boy not fire because of a malfunction of his gun? Or was he injured? Was he too far away to be heard? Maybe he hadn't thought to do so. With no new revelations to make a difference, I knew it was time to put my better half to work.

Leaving the trailer I glanced once again at the missing boy's mother and knew why I had been avoiding her eyes. The pain. Her face was contorted with fear and sadness, more than I could handle at the moment. Someone had an arm around her and I could hear him saying something like "this fresh dog is our best bet at finding him fast."

I hurried out of the trailer. I didn't want her to see my insecurity.

Conditions outdoors were ridiculous and worsening. I could not imagine a dog picking up and holding a scent in the howling wind. The snow was whipping my face so hard I needed goggles. Shielding my face with my hand, I hurried to the truck and opened the door. Michelle was raring to go. Weather or no weather, she was dying for action. That lifted my spirits and popped me into gear.

"OK" was her cue to leave the car, which she did by leaping high into the air and landing at a dead run in the clearing between the trailers. She then proceeded to run and jump as she snapped at snowflakes.

Nevil yelled over the wind, "How old is she?"

"A young adult," I yelled back as I grabbed my gear and headed toward the command trailer. Once inside, everyone hushed and crowded back, giving Michelle space. This created an awkward moment. I pinched Michelle in the rear and barked at her. She jumped, I laughed and the tension was broken. Everyone relaxed and we got down to business.

Nevil brought out the scent article, which was in a plastic bag and had been furnished by the boy's mother. It was yesterday's underpants, which Chris had left next to his bed. His mom said no one but her had touched the pants until she gave them to Nevil in the bag. Normally I would scent Michelle off an article only once. But under these conditions, I wanted to do it twice— once inside the trailer with no wind and again outside in the elements.

As I pulled my Gore-Tex rainsuit on over my jacket and dressed Michelle in her water-resistant, wool-lined coat, I was introduced to Duane, a volunteer fireman. Duane was going to accompany me, carrying radio and water and, hopefully, keeping *us* from getting lost. He was familiar with the woods but said, "It's pretty hard to tell where you are in this storm, everything looks so different."

He did not look happy. One more quick review of the map and sections already searched, one more quick radio check, and we were off. Except for one thing. I had requested that Chris's mother and Nevil be present when I scented Michelle off the underpants. The bag holding the pants would smell from both the mother and Nevil so I wanted them next to the bag when Michelle took her sniff. This way she could rule out two of the smells right away because she had already "found" them. They were right there.

Standing by the closed door of the trailer, I called Michelle over and told her to "Go find" as Nevil, Chris's mom and I held the open bag under her nose. Her response was perfect. She snorted the contents, brushed her nose by the mother, who gasped, then gently stuck her nose into Nevil's thigh just as I opened the trailer door.

Before I had descended the two trailer steps to the ground, I was hit by what felt like gale-force winds. The edge of the woods was only two hundred feet away but two hundred feet in such a storm made our mission seem impossible. I knew I couldn't hear anything, I couldn't see anything and I felt like I would be freezing to death within minutes. I didn't believe that a dog could work in these conditions and my only hope was that the woods would mute the wind and bring the noise down to a tolerable, workable level.

Fifty paces into the woods and my wish was granted— the world was quiet and calm with snow falling as on a postcard. While the tops of the trees were creaking and bending wildly, Michelle and I were in a winter wonderland. I opened the plastic bag once again, called Michelle over, lifted the underpants out, held them under her nose and said again, "Go find!"

She took a polite sniff and pranced away, nose to the ground. The red glow necklace that I'd hung around her neck for easy visibility seemed to take on a life of its own as it floated away. The bouncing red showed me Michelle was working but she was also enjoying the woods. Darting about, she would sniff a rock then check out a tree, getting the feel of the woods as she went. This is investigative work by the dog, a mental recording of the smells common to the area in preparation for recognizing when a new and different presence is smelled.

My plan was for us to head in a general southerly direction covering a very large grid, unless Michelle compelled us to follow a different heading. So far, she had nothing and we were meandering our way south. The air was filled with huge heavy wet snowflakes that stuck. The trees were tall and well spaced with little ground scrub to hamper us. A fairy-tale forest with the memory of the howling wind overhead, the white snow on the ground was unmarked by any trail, not even a deer had crossed this way. After a while, I found the sameness of trees and snow so unnerving that I began checking my compass compulsively to be sure we weren't going in circles.

I also kept looking up. I'd heard what sounded like big trees snapping in the distance, while overhead there was a cacophony of branches struggling against the strong gusts of wind. After one compass check that showed us heading more west than south, I whistled and pointed left at the same time that I angled my body left. Michelle was about fifty feet ahead and to the right, difficult to see through the falling snow, but she acknowledged the whistle and immediately changed direction. As she broke into a working lope with her nose to the ground, I was alarmed at how hard it was to keep her in view. "You need more glow necklaces, Michelle," I called, tension in my voice. "Come here!"

It wasn't until she approached me that I realized why she was so hard to see: except for her black nose and eyes, her coat was completely white from the wet snow. It certainly didn't bother her as she came at us prancing like a proud stallion and so comical in her all-white costume that I had to laugh. I looked back at Duane to see if he saw it, too. Then I really laughed. Duane looked like a two-legged Michelle! He, too, was white from head to toe except for his eyes, the only part of him not covered by clothing. I must have looked exactly the same because we all ended up laughing heartily. Michelle must have decided it was party time, too, because she pawed into the snow for a stick and came up with a piece of rotten wood, which she tossed into the air several times while barking.

Then, all of a sudden, there was one of those pauses like when you take a deep breath after a long laugh and no one says anything. We were all of us very quiet and quiet from within.

That's when we heard the woods singing. I looked up. I could hear music and a male voice singing. But all I could see through the haze of falling snow were treetops. They were bent to the point where something had to give. As I watched, a sudden wind gust whirled down from the trees to the ground a few feet away and then, in whirlpools of air and snow, blew over us. And as it passed by, we could hear with unmistakable clarity the sound of a Gregorian chant. I was so stunned that I plopped down into a sitting position in the snow, unceremonious but safe. I looked up at Duane.

"Holy shit," he said, then tumbled into the snow beside me. Neither of us spoke for the next few seconds.

"Wind spirits, man," said Duane, keeping his voice low. "My grandfather told me about the spirits in the wind. If you spend enough time in the woods and you're lucky, you'll meet one. That was a wind spirit, man."

I was too dumbfounded to speak, plus I didn't know what to say. All I knew for sure was that something had happened. I looked around for Michelle. When I saw what she was doing, I wanted to scream. But hyperventilating and on the verge of throwing up, I couldn't make a sound.

Michelle was vertical, literally walking and hopping on two legs, totally erect and with her nose as high as it would go. As she walked among the trees—in that strange, unnatural position—I kept losing sight of her behind the trees.

After a few seconds, I found my voice and managed to squeak out her name. No response. Then I saw her. She was continuing to walk and hop like some alien "dog man" until she was out of sight.

I scrambled to my feet, yelling. Before I could move forward, I saw movement in the trees. Thank God it was Michelle, bounding toward me on all fours. Relief rushed over me. And when she got to me, we were a study in opposites: she was happy, I was very shaken.

"Wind spirits?" I said over my shoulder to Duane. "Did you see my dog?"

"Does she do that a lot?" he asked. "That was damn weird."

"Never," I said. "I've never seen anything like that. I thought I was hallucinating and . . . it scared the shit out of me."

Duane's face was whiter than the snow falling around us. The look in his eyes was a cross between fear and confusion. "What was that about? Why and how did she do that?"

"I think that whatever we heard, Michelle heard. She also smelled it, saw it and sensed it in a way that we can't begin to understand. And it was so compelling to her that it caused her to walk upright. My guess is that her face was right in it at that height."

"Jeez," said Duane. Then we were both quiet, reflecting. Though it wasn't really quiet around us. The trees were chanting: snap, twist, pop, groan, crack. "I'll tell you, man," said Duane, "this is walking on the edge!"

I knew we were both hoping not to hear another sound/crash. That's when I saw Michelle standing a few feet away and staring at me with eyes twinkling over her slack-mouth smile. Talk about pet therapy, her message was clear.

"Listen, Duane," I said. "As far as I'm concerned, whatever was there was good. Michelle loved it. She came back happy and look at her now. She's having the time of her life, and she's telling us it's time to get back to work."

With that, I took two more glow necklaces from an inside pocket and called Michelle over. I chose blue and red, activated them, and hung them around her neck. "Now I'll be able to see you because, once again, you're nuclear dog." As I spoke I pinched her rear playfully. Jumping and frolicking, she was eager to get back to the hunt.

We headed into the same course as before, SSW. After an hour or so, my neck was aching from looking up so much, but trees and branches were coming down all over the place as the sound of their breaking and falling escalated.

Then Duane said something I'll never forget: "This is a symphony, man, and we're right in the middle of the woodwind section." I found his words exhilarating until I realized we were also at the mercy of treachery from above.

We moved on, still on the same heading. I radioed in what I thought was our position and the fact that Michelle had not yet picked up a scent. Just then two large branches fell much too close, one immediately in front of and one right behind us. It was nerve-wracking. Michelle was jumpy, too. She was covering a lot of ground and I imagined it must have looked like a minefield to her. She was out of sight most of the time and I worried when I heard her yelp after a loud crack from the trees. But when I called, she came and a quick check showed her to be fine.

About an hour after that, I noticed a subtle change in the movement of her glow necklaces. Usually, in the dark, they look like magic rings floating through the forest—but the rings weren't floating anymore, they were darting!

"Hold it," I said, the adrenaline rush charging through me.

"What?" said Duane, hearing the excitement in my voice.

"Michelle's got something."

This is the moment you wait for, the *alert*. This is where the game really begins. I headed toward her darting lights. They continued to dart. When I was within her earshot, I said, "What ya got? Hey, nuclear dog, you got something?" She registered my words with a hop and a skip while happily working the wind.

"Where is he, girl?" I stood perfectly still, not wanting to lead her in any direction, and waited. But not for long. She was moving fast and in a definite direction, quartering back and forth, always working the wind.

I was very excited . . . then the doubt set in. With every search this happens: a quick chill of terror sneaks into my heart. What if she's just crittering, following the scent of an animal? What if I'm reading her wrong . . . what if . . . what if . . . ? Then, as I always do, I admonish myself: Trust the dog, trust the dog.

Michelle was soon moving so far ahead of us that I lost sight of her glow rings. We kept moving as fast as we could in the direction she was going and waited for her to show herself again. After five minutes, she came back to check in with me, but this time again there was a difference from the norm. She came all the way back to me, which is usually a great sign because she'll come right up to me, then pick up a stick. Only this time she didn't pick up a stick. She just danced around me, then headed back out to where she had been.

"Can you translate that for me?" asked Duane.

"I'm not sure. I thought for a moment that she had lost the scent. But that's not the case, she's back on it now. I don't know what she's saying. Maybe the scent is weak and she came back for reassurance."

Things continued this way for a while; Michelle worked and we followed. The wind in the treetops let up a little and we didn't have to look up as often, but at our feet the wind was skimming flecks of ice off the ground. The snowfall continued heavy. We entered an area of the forest where the trees were much older, bigger and spaced farther apart. Tired, we stopped to rest. Not much was said. I was mulling over the "spirit in the wind" and the unforgettable sight of Michelle disappearing into the woods erect on her hind legs. I'll never get over that sight.

But Michelle was antsy with our resting and so were we. It was too darn cold to sit around. But just as we headed out, Michelle suddenly circled back, cut in front of Duane and stopped. He nearly tripped over her.

"What the hell?" He stumbled sideways. "What was that about, Michelle?" He started to walk around her. She leaped in front of him and started barking. Duane backed off, shocked and not a little afraid that she was about to attack him. I was shocked, too. I had never seen her display such unjustified aggression toward a person.

"Leave it!" I yelled and ran toward the two of them. Duane froze but Michelle stood there placidly, wagging her stump tail and looking at me as if to say, "What's all the running about?"

"Your dog is crazy, man," said Duane

I didn't know what to say. I called to Michelle, "Come here," and started to back up in order to move her away from Duane. Now she barked and jumped at me! But she didn't hit me, she landed next to me, maybe a little behind, but looking me in the eye and barking. That's when I realized it was not an aggressive bark but a furious one. She's telling me something, I said to myself.

"What is it?" I got down on my knees to look her in the face. "What is it, M?"

She took a step back and pawed at the ground while barking into my face. I was dumbfounded but loving it. "She's telling me something, she's found something—I just have to figure it out," I said to Duane.

Now she was pawing the ground with both paws while jumping up and down on her front legs. The she started to disappear *right in front of my eyes*. She pawed the ground in front of her and her foot went down, followed by the other foot, then her chest and her head. Only her big rump was visible before I realized she was falling into a chasm! I grabbed and got my right arm around her rear legs and groin and was reaching for her collar when I knew I was going in myself. Right then I felt the strong grip of Duane on my jacket shoulder. He held on while I got Michelle up safely.

"Holy shit, hooooolceee shit! It's a hole, a cloud-hole, a hole filled with snow!" I said.

"Yeah, but the snow's so light and powdery—it's cloud-like, almost like a trap," said Duane.

"A trap? Duane, don't go paranoid on me now."

"Well, this is pretty weird. The whole night's been damn weird. It's been the craziest night of my life, way beyond bizarre," he said loudly. Then he lowered his voice as he nodded in Michelle's direction, "She saved my life."

"What do you think this is?" I gestured toward the hole.

Duane stepped back, pushed back his hood, took off his baseball hat, scratched his head as he inhaled deeply, then he said, "Foundation."

"You mean like a cement foundation for a house?"

"Yup. Let's get out of here."

I didn't need any convincing. We gave that cloud-hole a wide berth.

We had been pushing on for nearly another hour when Michelle suddenly cruised by, lightly brushing my leg. Preoccupied with the events of our hike, I didn't notice at first. I was mesmerized by a strange pall over the woods and a deepening sense of foreboding. Then it dawned on me—that physical contact from Michelle. It was not a random happening, she doesn't do that unless she has a reason.

I snapped to and looked for her. I realized that she hadn't just brushed by, she had deliberately touched the scent article hanging in the bag at my waist. Finally I saw her. She was working! Within two minutes, Michelle confirmed to me that she was working the lost boy's scent. Again, she returned, touched the scent article with her nose, then headed out to quarter an area.

But the direction changed! She had us heading due south now, not SSW. My heart started pounding as the glow rings changed from her slow, methodical back-and-forth to a more rapid darting. The pattern remained the same and I came to understand what her changing presentation meant: whenever she had a hint of the boy's scent in the wind, she darted; when she had nothing, she worked the slower pattern in order to find something, anything.

Over the next twenty minutes I could see the relationship between her darts and the wind gusts. Every so often, on an especially strong gust, she would do a little two-step hop and dart for a few seconds. I found myself hoping for wind gusts. Then, even though she lost it when the wind died, she continued to work enthusiastically, buoyed by the "strokes" she received. The strokes were the actual experience of smelling the scent particles of the boy and my generous praise.

Now that we had something, we radioed in that Michelle was showing excitement in a southerly direction. Duane relayed what he estimated to be our location. Then we had another fifteen minutes of that pattern of darting, then slowing, a trace of fresh scent, then nothing.

I called the search commander to let him know the kid was still a distance away. "Michelle is telling me not to get too excited, we've got a ways to go," I said. Then I asked, "Do you have any search teams south of us?"

"Two—one east of you and one west, southwest of you. They both started at the edge of a gorge so it's doubtful the boy is south of them," he said.

"Great! Have the west group fan north and east and have the east group fan north and west—"

"Right, maybe we can find him with a pincer grid," the search commander interrupted. Since all the searchers' radios were on the same wavelength, everyone heard our conversation. Both units responded and headed toward us as we followed Michelle's nose south. The east party had a newly arrived dog, the west did not. They were a small group of firemen on foot.

We hadn't gone ten minutes before we heard a tremendous clatter from the radio. I thought I heard someone say, ". . . child's voice." Then seconds later more excited voices all talking at the same time made any words unintelligible. At last we heard, "We got him!"

Duane and I stopped to listen. My heart was pounding again as we waited. "He's somewhat hypothermic but okay . . . we're giving him heated oxygen and transporting . . . he's conscious and verbal. . . ." I turned to shake Duane's hand but he grabbed me in a bear hug and spun us both around, shouting, "Your dog did it, man!"

With the relief the boy was found came the recognition that I had been frightened. Now that the pressure of "find" was off, I let myself feel how uncomfortable I was. If Duane hadn't been there to share the weird experiences, I might have feared for my sanity. As it was, I was still pretty shaky.

And I still had a minor problem—Michelle. She had done her job without actually making the find. Now she wanted to continue south and did not understand why it was time to head back to base camp. I didn't want to give her a "find" reward (stick play) without coming upon a person or at least an article of the person. So, as best I could, I redirected her back to base camp. She took my command reluctantly. This was not how it should work. Had we been closer to the victim and had she had a definitive scent cone, she would have dashed in for the actual find and returned with an article from the victim.

I knew what she needed as a result of some training I had done with Michelle and my wife. First, we arranged for Jaye to be lying down as if she was an unconscious victim. Then, when Michelle picked up a stick to tell me she had found Jaye, instead of giving her the refind command to bring me there, I pretended stupidity. I wanted to see what she would do.

Her response was marvelous. She disappeared but returned minutes later with Jaye's hat. As Jaye described it: "After she initially found me and I played dead, she left me to get you. When she returned a few minutes later, she sniffed me intently, gave a loud bark right in my ear, then snatched my hat and ran off."

Remembering that episode now, I radioed ahead and asked that any article the boy might have on his body right now be left at the edge of the woods in a predetermined spot. A short while later, they radioed back that the article, his hat, would be about twenty feet off the northwest corner of a fire truck at base camp. Good.

Our walk back was long and tiring and it was still snowing hard. I was exhausted when we finally got to base camp. Actually, I smelled the gasoline fumes before I saw it or any lights. "I'm hanging out with Michelle too much," I muttered.

As we headed in, I directed us toward the fire truck so that Michelle could find the hat. She did a beautiful job.

When I got through with her, she was the proudest dog. We didn't just have stick play to celebrate—I rolled on the ground with her. We wrestled. I praised her to the point that she burst into what some call a "frap period." That's when the dog dashes around like a nut, like a young pup. So there we were—I was as exhausted from fright as from physical effort and she was running around like an idiot. I loved it. As far as Michelle was concerned, we had had a successful and fun night. The best motivation for our next search.

*   *   *

Epilogue:

The boy was fine. His mother fainted with relief when she heard he had been found and was okay.

I was greeted warmly by the other searchers, one of whom said, "God bless you for your efforts!" Meanwhile, I was feeling elated, wide awake and eager to get home and tell my story.

Nevil, the search commander, was nowhere in sight, so I jumped into my truck and headed home. Though we made it by 7 A.M., it wasn't easy. Snow froze on the windshield, forcing me to run the defroster full blast, except when I had to redirect the heat to keep my feet from freezing! When I redirected heat away from the windshield, I could only drive a short distance before having to pull over to chip ice off the exterior of the windshield.

Michelle, meanwhile, snored blissfully. It was so cold and miserable that I couldn't stand listening to her. This so irritated me, I woke her up twice to discuss what I still consider the strangest search we've ever been on. And I never saw Duane again.

Training Notes

My Secret Lure

I had never heard of the woman who called me at the crack of dawn that morning.

"Who is this?" I asked, struggling to wake up. I could see the hands on the clock in a vertical line, straight up and down and blinking, as if to say, "too early for this."

"What is it?" asked my wife, sounding scared.

I covered the mouthpiece, "A dog call."

"Tell him to call later and hang up." Jaye rolled over, hoping for a few more minutes of sleep before the alarm went off.

But the young woman, Dina, was not going to be put off. "My employer needs help," she said. That got my attention; most people start talking about their dog.

"Your employer?"

"Yes, I'm sorry for calling so early but my boss, Mr. Jurgens, said I couldn't wait. His dog got out of the house and won't come in and Mr. Jurgens can't leave for work with Abigail in the front yard."

"What kind of dog is this and how old?" I asked, still enjoying the warmth and comfort of my bed.

"A Welsh terrier and I think she's three, maybe four years old."

"Where is she now?"

"On the front lawn. Mr. Jurgens has been trying to get her in all night and he's very upset."

"Has he tried using food to lure her in?"

"Yes, yes, everything. Can you get her in the house now?" The young woman sounded desperate. I realized I was enjoying the conversation immensely because I knew exactly what was needed to lure a manipulative terrier into a house and I hadn't even sat up in bed yet.

"Where are you located?"

She told me. "I'll be there in thirty minutes."

I pulled up about forty minutes later. The address was in a very affluent neighborhood and this home was particularly formidable with a huge cast-iron gate and ten-foot high stone pillars fronting a high stucco wall circling the property. I was waiting in front of the gate looking for an intercom or something that would let me in when a disembodied voice asked, "Are you the dog trainer?"

"Tom Shelby," I answered.

The gate swung open and the voice said, "Follow the road to the main house."

As I drove up toward an enormous stone-and-brick home, my eye was drawn to the second step of the large front stoop. There, in slippers, black socks, suit pants and a yellow pajama top, sat someone who had to be Mr. Jurgens. Actually, it was Mr. Jurgens and the entire contents of his refrigerator.

Forty feet away lay Abigail. Basking in the glow of the newly risen sun.

I pulled into the circular drive and angled my car at a diagonal to the front door, careful not to park in front of it. Then I got out of my car and walked toward Abigail, talking lovingly, trying to con her into thinking we were friends.

She didn't buy it for a second. As I approached, she started to get up. So I stepped back and sat down on the grass, which is a friendly invitation in dog language. Her mouth opened in a smile and her tail wagged lazily but her face said, "Nice try but I wasn't born yesterday. If hot dogs couldn't get me in, do you think I'm going to fall for your sitting down?"

That's what I had expected, but I wanted to give it a try anyway. I stood up and headed for Mr. Jurgens. He was still on the stoop, watching. Short and stocky with a long face and scraggly beard, he did not look happy. I, on the other hand, felt great because I knew I could get Abigail into the house whenever I wanted, and I was thoroughly enjoying keeping Mr. Jurgens in suspense. I looked past him at the display of Brie cheese, artichokes and other food staples.

"Having a sidewalk sale of pre-owned food?"

"I hope you brought more than a sense of humor to get the dog into the house." He didn't smile.

"Would you like me to get her in right now?"

He looked at me with a bleak expression on his face.

I turned to the car and whistled. A head appeared at the open back window.

"OK, Michelle." Michelle leaped out the window and headed toward me with only the slightest glance sideways at Abigail. By the time she reached me and Mr. Jurgens, Abigail was beside herself with territorial response.

All dogs have a strong territorial response to other dogs coming onto their property. Add to that the fact that a terrier is the type of dog that looks in a mirror and sees God. I barely had time to get Michelle past the stoop and into the house before Abigail came flying over the stoop in a single bound. She was airborne at over eighty miles an hour, legs churning so fast that she skidded across the tile floor into a shelf, which exploded, showering bric-a-brac everywhere.

I quickly ushered Michelle out of the house and told her to wait. Then I closed the door and turned to Mr. Jurgens. Abigail was standing in the mess in the hallway, barking. "Sorry about the shelf," I said. "You know, with a little training I could teach her 'Quiet' in addition to better manners."

Maybe I was a little cocky over my success but I was taken aback when he responded curtly, "I was expecting some dog trainer magic, but not this."

"Sir, the magic was first—knowing to use a dog— and second, having a dog to make it so easy."

I collected my fee and headed home for more sleep. The entire episode took less than five minutes. In spite of Jurgens's cool manner, I laughed all the way home.

That guy may give orders to more than a thousand people, but he sure couldn't manage Abigail.

5

Blood on the Windshield

Every search starts with the ringing of my phone but this is too much: 7:30 A.M. on a Saturday at my country house. Who the hell is calling me here? This is the only place I'm able to sleep late, sometimes as late as 10. By the third ring, I'm more than halfway out of bed. We don't have a bedside phone at the country house, mainly because my family is always here with me so anxiety levels are low. There's no worrying where the kids are.

By the fourth ring, I'm in the hall. Jaye and the kids are still asleep so I figure maybe it's a wrong number. Maybe there's a problem with Jaye's mom? On the fifth ring, I grab it and squawk a sleepy, "Hello?"

"*You* sound great," the voice on the other end chuckles. "Did I catch you in the middle of exercising?"

"Frank." As well as being a member of the Amigo team, he's one of my best buddies, and, definitely, a practical joker. What he is not is a voice I want to hear at the crack of dawn. "Since you asked, I just finished my six-mile run and was in the middle of my aerobics routine when so rudely interrupted. What's up?"

I was very pleased with my answer—not bad for a guy whose first word was a squawk.

"We got a search over in Phoenecia. Car hit a tree, blood on the windshield and the driver is missing."

Frank's words took a while to register. A search was the last thing I expected on this warm August Saturday. I was mumbling something unintelligible when Frank cut me off. "Pick you up in fifteen minutes."

"Thirty," I bargained while hanging up. But I heard his phone click off even as I spoke.

Still in a haze, I did a couple 360s before I could figure out what to do next. Michelle, curled up in her beanbag chair, was kind enough to acknowledge me by opening one eye. Above that one eye was a brow furrowed with the obvious question: Why aren't you back in bed?

"You'll find out soon enough," I said. This brought her head up, both eyes open.

Twenty minutes later, mentally and equipment-challenged due to being half asleep still, I somehow managed to get Michelle and myself into Frank's car.

"You look terrible," said Frank.

I smiled wanly. "You would, too, if you were looking at what I'm looking at—at this hour of the morning. I don't know how your wife does it." I shook my head. Actually, Frank is a little over six feet tall and ruggedly good-looking. Both Frank and his wife, Debbie, are close friends of ours.

A soft whine came from the backseat. Michelle, on

this day, is nearly three years old and weighs in at seventy-six pounds. She is in the prime of her Doberman life and always impatient when it comes to manhunting. That's what this really is, this K-9 SAR work: manhunting with a dog. And I love it almost as much as Michelle does.

"Ok, what's the rap?" I asked.

"Farmer on his tractor at daybreak found the car imbedded in a tree, hair and blood on the windshield, which was cracked from the inside—no driver. Farmer said the car wasn't there last night when he left the fields. The strange thing is that the owner of the car, a Donald Eames, age twenty, called his mother at two-thirty in the morning and told her he was OK and that he was calling from outside the post office and would be home soon. Then he hung up. He didn't mention anything about a car accident and—here's the strange part—*there is no phone outside the post office.*

"Eddie is already at the site with Abu. He wanted to get there as soon as possible to stop police and firemen from contaminating the area for the dogs. He'll probably take over the whole show."

Ed is an excellent dog trainer, and he and I were training Frank and Yogi, Frank's Bernese mountain dog, to be an SAR unit. Ed, who hails from the South Bronx and is a counselor at the nearby juvenile correction facility, is also a good friend.

The ride to Phoenecia would take half an hour. "You bring any breakfast?" I asked. I could smell coffee.

"Behind me on the floor." Frank pointed over his shoulder. I spotted a Dunkin' Donuts bag.

"Ah, my favorite health food."

For the next twenty minutes, Frank drove and

yawned; I ate and watched the landscape fly by. Lost in thought as we prepared ourselves for the search, we were quiet. I found myself wiping sweat from my forehead and realized the day was going to be a hot one. Before long we were in Phoenecia, where the streets were empty, desolate.

Frank chuckled, doing his Rod Serling imitation: "We've just entered the Twilight Zone and this is Ghosttown." Relaxed and easy in our early-morning mind-set, we were still enjoying that little fantasy when we turned onto Main Street. The sight ahead reminded us of the very real task that lay ahead.

In the middle of the block was the old firehouse. A small crowd of men had gathered there. Frank parked and walked over to the group while I stayed in the car. It was getting hotter by the minute and sunlight already shimmered off the cracked and frost-heaved slabs of concrete sidewalk. The buildings around the firehouse looked weatherworn and in need of paint. Even the crowd of men looked old. I found the sight oddly depressing and started to get anxious.

Finally, Frank got back into the car. "Christ, it's hot out there," he said.

"You bullshit with those guys for half an hour and that's all you got to say—it's hot?"

"We got another half hour to ride," said Frank as he pulled out, made a U-turn on Main Street and fell in behind a state trooper heading out to the search site. As soon as we pulled out of town, the state trooper turned on his flashers and pressed down on the accelerator. Frank whooped like a banshee and stayed right on his tail. No doubt about it: speeding with impunity is exhilarating. It had to be an odd sight with us appearing to be chasing the police car!

I was glad and not a little relieved to arrive alive at the search command post. This time we met up with a cluster of different types of vehicles with lots of flashing lights parked off to the left along the edge of a large field. Everyone was out of their vehicles and gathering in the shade of a grove of trees. The field itself was surrounded by what appeared to be impenetrable woods. Across the road from the field was more of the same, fields of hay surrounded by trees and mountains.

Frank and I were both out of the car almost before it stopped moving. That Indy 500 with the state trooper was just what we needed to wake up. As I exited the car, I told Michelle to wait, that I would be back soon and then we would go to work. She knows what "wait," "soon" and "work" mean and jumped into the front seat, impatient, as I walked off with Frank.

I left the car door open on purpose. It's a quick way of getting Michelle the respect she deserves. Walking up to the group, I knew this would be more fun than usual when I heard one guy say, "Ohmygod, it's a Dobe. Those dogs scare me." Once we got to the group and I was comfortable with the setup, I turned back toward the car and called out, "OK." Michelle leaped from the car like a long jumper for the track team and ran at us full-speed. I've seen her do this a thousand times, but I was still impressed. When it comes to work, Michelle's enthusiasm is intense.

I could feel the men behind me shift nervously as she came running at us. That's when I said in a loud, firm voice, "Don't kill." Then I turned to the shaken crowd behind me and said, "You guys are okay now. She won't do anything now that she's got the 'don't kill' command." All but one got the joke and smiled. The one who didn't glared. Michelle, meanwhile, came to a screeching halt in front of me with a huge smile on her face. She's so funny. When she's extremely happy she smiles what I call her slack jaw smile. Her mouth is so wide open, she looks a little silly. This was one of those times so I said to her happily, "You look like an idiot, hurry up."

"Hurry up" is my command for her to go to the bathroom, to "make." And so she did, promptly exploring the immediate area and relieving herself.

This, by the way, is a great command, easy to teach and very pragmatic, yet few dog owners bother to teach it. Some older dogs have learned on their own to relieve themselves anytime they get outdoors, but many dogs don't know. Imagine the hassle of arriving at your friend's boat after a three-hour drive with your dog, you're late, everyone wants to leave right away but your dog is too distracted to go to the bathroom. You know that Bowser won't get the opportunity again for another six or seven hours because you'll be on the darn boat. But if I've been your trainer, you can say, "Hold on, everyone, while I command Bowser to make, unless you plan for him to make on the boat." With everyone looking on, Bowser will make and you'll look great in the process.

While Michelle was taking care of business, I noticed my friend Eddie had taken charge of the SAR effort and was talking to a state trooper. I was relieved. I didn't particularly feel like being in charge that day. If I'm the only K-9 unit on the scene that automatically makes me the expert and means I'm in charge. Little do people know I'm figuring it all out as I go along.

But with this many people, things get more complicated. Right now Eddie was answering lots of questions, making decisions for the group and basically handling the social politics of the scene. This always happens when you have a number of individuals involved. I'll never forget my arrival at a search scene where I walked into a caustic argument between a local cop and a state trooper. Those two had history and the result was a search hampered by excessive and unnecessary politics. Neither knew anything about search dogs, both wanted me on their side. That stuff I can do without.

Today it was Eddie's problem. Great. I had another cup of coffee and schmoozed with a few of the guys while I waited for Ed to go over the map with me.

Michelle did the same except for the coffee—schmoozed with Ed's dog, Abu. Actually, they were playing wildly, dive-bombing each other and play fighting. Instrumental in intensifying Michelle's working drive and hardwiring her powerful work ethic, Abu has been a mentor to Michelle since she was a pup. She did this through her own love of the hunt.

Abu was an older dog and already working seriously when the two dogs met. At the time Michelle was just a small pup and ideal for use as a training "distraction." From the start, Michelle was acutely aware of Abu's focus and possessive guarding of her working space. Abu was always tolerant of the younger dog's rough play, but if Abu was told to "go find" and Michelle interfered in any way, she was immediately and roughly cut to size by Abu—learning the hard way that working time is to be coveted.

Ed's chat session over, he sauntered my way with a

map that would define my search grid. We decided to scent the dogs off the car seat since the car was found unlocked. I was given one very old map of the area and one very rough hand-drawn sketch of current landmarks. That was it: scent off the car seat and a less-than-accurate map of the area.

We hoped that one of the dogs would pick up the actual foot trail of Donald Eames, assuming the registered owner of the car had been the driver. Then . . . follow the dog. Trust the dog.

Trust the dog—the axiom of K-9 SAR.

The search team was made up of six other men besides Frank, Ed, myself and the two dogs. Ed and I agreed that the six men would search as three two-man units, Frank would coordinate and dispatch from the command post, and Ed and I would go it alone with our dogs. This is not prudent and we knew it: it is always smarter to have a partner. But we are experienced searchers. After all, Ed, Frank and I spent two years establishing Amigo Search and Rescue as a certified K-9 unit. In its infancy, Amigo was too small to have partners ("co-ops" as we call them)—it was always just the three of us, our dogs and the mountains.

In this case, the advantage to going it alone would be the ability to cover more territory. If we didn't do it this way, if Ed and I each had a co-op, then there would be only two other two-man units to search. Also, Ed had just received word that two more Amigo SAR units would arrive within the hour. So the plan seemed very reasonable.

We were ready. Our adrenaline levels were high. They say the most exciting moments of a prizefight are the three seconds before, during and after the bell rings.

Same goes for those three seconds before, during and after I say, "Go find." It's a moment of truth.

Suddenly it was time. Standing ten feet apart, Ed and I spoke simultaneously, calling, "Abu," and "Michelle!" The dogs immediately stopped their play and came, and it would have looked very impressive if they had gone to the right people. Instead, Michelle screeched to a halt in the heel position in front of Ed. Abu slid to a stop right in front of me. We were stunned. I think we both felt a little ridiculous. We started ranking on the dogs.

"Ranking" is a critical exercise used to correct a dog. If done right, the bond between you and the dog grows closer at the same time that you both understand the error. It is one of those times when "it's not what you say but how you say it" and can open up a whole new world of communication with your dog.

Ranking is how—with a light dose of sarcasm—I tell Michelle that I love her, I love to communicate with her like this, that I respect her, that we're both having a good time and her screwup was very funny. This little exercise is identical to bantering with a buddy when one of you has screwed up and you can kid about it . . . while still ranking on one another.

"Michelle! Are you blind or what?" said Ed, doing his own ranking. "Do I look like a white boy to you?"

Our dogs responded with huge super smiles on their faces. I had to crack up. Do I think these dogs are smart enough to understand on a subconscious level that they have just made a mistake? Do they know they have just been caught sitting in front of the wrong pack leader? Do they know that our reactions are confirming their mistakes yet bringing it into the open so that they can correct their actions? You bet they do.

That's the easy part. The challenge is to know how to rank in a way that you correct while strengthening your bond with the dog. My dog loves the way I communicate with her—and the more she loves our mutual communication, the more she understands. I like to describe this as my "dog boy's tunnel into dog humor."

While Ed and I ranked, Michelle and Abu changed places. I'm convinced they wised up at the same time they felt closer to us: heard our ranking, felt our love.

Ten minutes later, after commandeering Frank's car, Michelle and I arrived where we would start our search. In search lingo, it was time to "clear our grid."

Ed and Frank and I had made the decision to "go grids" earlier when it was obvious that the area around the car had been so contaminated by searchers that the dogs could not pick up a scent trail. Both Abu and Michelle had been given similar commands after sniffing the car seat: "Good girl! This is the person we're going to have to 'go find.' " We gave the command in excited voices that emphasized "Go find!" Then both dogs were maneuvered into widening circles around the car until it was obvious they could scent nothing. Thus the grids.

To do that, I had Michelle take another scenting off the car seat but this time I spoke to her differently, not wanting her to go into an immediate search mode as soon as she left the car. This time she had to note the driver's smell and hold on to that olfactory memory until we reached our starting point, our assigned grid. My command this time: "Hey, search dog, smell this and go find—but not right now—be patient." As I spoke and Michelle was checking out the seat, I was up close and talking in a monotone laced with tinges of excitement. Several times she heard the key words "go find." I also rubbed the car seat with a tissue in case we had to spend the night in the woods. The tissue would hold the scent and remind Michelle the next day of the person we were looking for. She understood.

She was also patient. Patience is a two-way street. My patience with her enhances the bond between us at the same time that it teaches her to be patient with me. She is patient, too, because she knows that she is about to be rewarded with a search. This is similar to placing a treat on a dog's nose and telling the dog not to eat until you say, "OK." Easy to do because the dog is looking at an imminent reward.

Two steps out of the car and the sun felt like a hammer. I looked into an expanse of scrub brush and field that stretched as far as I could see. Uninviting, the terrain was thorny and swampy. Much as I hated to leave the road, I plunged in. The fields that had looked so clean from a distance were scrubby up close. Lots of waist-high thorny bushes, brambles, small trees, difficult to traverse in many spots, I found it hard to maintain a southeast course. At one point, I had to drop back a quarter mile northwest in order to find some way through the branches ripping and tearing through my clothes. It was the dead opposite way I wanted to go but the only way to get there without bleeding too much. Michelle, meanwhile, was throroughly enjoying herself! It's amazing how she can whiz right through thorns without getting shredded. A Doberman's face and body is built for this kind of work. I can't imagine a poor pug trying this—that little dog with its flat face and bulging eyes would need an EMT after a stroll through this brush.

A human shouldn't be here either—unless dropped in

by parachute or wandering with a severe head injury.

Michelle was now crittering. The area was rife with animal scent, with scat everywhere. Usually, if a search dog follows animal trails instead of looking for human beings, the dog is not trustworthy and should be washed out of any SAR training program. But even though Michelle was having a great time with all the fresh animal scents, I wasn't concerned. I knew she'd work when the time was right.

If in the course of happy exploring she comes across the scent of a human, she'll respond instantly. We've had this experience several times. Once a deer came crashing through the woods, startling both of us, then disappeared in three bounds. In spite of my consternation and multiple "leave it" commands, Michelle toyed with the deer's trail for a while. But in one instant, on scenting a human, she stiffened, pointed her nose straight into the wind, made a ninety-degree turn and she was off working.

Right now she was having fun while I fought my way through scrub brush hell. After an hour, the landscape changed. The small trees disappeared and we were in a giant field of knee- to waist-high grass and hay. This appeared to be an abandoned hayfield. The heat was more oppressive now, as if those little trees had at least furnished some shade. I could see a forest in the distance and all I focused on was getting there and getting some real shade.

Tall grass isn't the easiest to traverse in heat. It holds hot moist air, which is released when the grass is parted. In order to stay on my southeast course, I had a good half mile to walk before reaching the edge of the woods, and by now I was sweating so profusely that I had to stop to wipe my sunglasses every few minutes.

I noticed something else I had never seen before, a curious reflection through my sunglasses: the high grasses appeared to be filled with glinting baskets of spun silver. I stopped and leaned down to inspect the lovely visions. Whoa! Each basket was a spider web holding a very large, very ugly spider. I was horrified. Horrified and a half mile to go. I had to walk through the damn things and they were everywhere! I found it absolutely impossible to avoid brushing against them. The experience was so revolting that it was one of the few times in my entire K-9 SAR career that I have questioned my sanity in "doing this shit."

Michelle, of course, couldn't care less as she cruised through the little buggers, covered with spider webs. I have to admit this was one time when the adult in me had a very hard time keeping the child in me from running in sheer panic. That remains the most miserable walk in a field I have ever made.

The woods were heaven. Elegant white pines stretched their branches a good twenty-five feet overhead and offered up a soft cushion of pine needles for my feet: real shade, no scrub, and, thank god, no spiders.

I radioed Ed.

After telling him our estimated distance traveled and course heading, I added that Michelle had found nothing. Since all the searchers had radios on the same band and could hear my message to Ed, I asked if anyone out there knew about the spiders. That was a mistake.

Someone from base camp radioed back right away. Even though our connection kept breaking up, I could hear enough: ". . . called field widows, related to black widows . . . love to get in at the cuff . . . probably up

your pants . . . don't let them . . . skin. . . ." And the radio went dead. I never heard of field widows and knew
that this would be a standing joke at my expense for
well into the future.

The radio didn't worry me nearly as much as the spiders. It had worked just fine a minute earlier and the
batteries were pretty fresh. I figured it must be interference at this location and would work again as soon as
we moved on. Meanwhile, the rough, very old map and
the nonfunctioning radio were all I had at the moment.
Not too comforting, but then again, it was early in the
day. I didn't have to worry about getting lost in the dark
and I could always retrace my steps heading northwest.
Sure, back through the spider field. Uh-huh.

Instead, Michelle and I continued to head southeast.
After about fifteen minutes, we emerged from the woods
to see a large farm in front of us: a picture-perfect white
farmhouse with a stand of spruce to the north, rolling
fields of varied crops all around, two silos, several barns,
corrals, horses and lots of cows. Picturesque though it
might be, I wanted to avoid it. Most farms have a dog
or two that might see Michelle as invading their turf.

Of course, at the same time I realized someone at the
farm might have seen someone wandering or be able to
give me other information. I decided that as soon as I
got out of the interference zone I would radio in and see
if someone at base camp could call the farm and check
it out. I wanted to stay with my grid and keep moving.

Even though I wanted to avoid the farm, it wasn't
easy. The only way around was to the right, opposite
my southeast course, and I would have to pass a little
too close to the house. Scratch that. Another option, to
the left, would mean cutting across one section of the

farmyard. That left a detour back through the woods. I decided on the detour. Not only would the woods be cooler but I would be much less apt to run into proprietary dogs.

Unfortunately, the detour stopped almost as soon as it started: a mucky swamp confronted us. This was no friendly swamp where you can leap from hillock to hillock, but the quicksand type, the suck-your-boot-off-with-every-step type. I was forced to head back toward the farm.

Hurrying back toward the fields, I soon found that the open areas were deceptively longer than they appeared and populated with a lot of cows. I kept Michelle close with "wait" and "stick around" commands. Part of her training had included exposure to cows and other farm animals so their presence didn't distract her, but she was aware and interested.

We were moving forward at a steady pace, minding our own business, when the cows took over. I wasn't aware of it at first. Then I felt a presence and another presence. Cows may look like dots when you see them from a car, but do you realize how huge a Holstein is up close? Enormous.

And we had dozens coming at us. They weren't charging, they were walking. But they weren't walking away, *they were walking at us*. From all across the field, with clear and deliberate intent, what seemed like thousands of cows were surrounding us. They came closer and closer. The scene was unnerving. Even Michelle was bristling, hackles up at the sight. And I don't think she even saw the ones approaching from the rear and on the outside flanks.

"Easy," I said, unsure what to do. But as the wall of

living steak closed in, I realized we had to make our bird. That's marine talk for "get the hell out of here!"

By now, I feared for Michelle's life. A few cows is one thing, this was hair-raising. She was clueless about a cow's kicking ability and even though (as I learned later from a farmer) the cows were only curious, this had become a fight or flight situation for me and my dog.

Suddenly, through a small opening in the wall of beef, I spotted a two-post fence, part of a large corral. "This way," I said. I waved my arms as I jogged toward the escape route. I was careful not to yell as I waved because that might incite Michelle. She was clearly delighted and responded instantly. Later I realized this was probably another one of those shared experiences when she picked up cues from me that I didn't even know I was giving. The cows did not block our path but gave way for us to make it to the fence. I hopped over and Michelle hopped through. Safe!

"Wasn't that fun?" I tried to sound happy as I lied to Michelle. Always training, dog guys like me do stuff like that—we want the experience to be fun, not traumatic. I dropped to my knees to praise her and play for a minute, then started across the corral to exit on the far side, away from what now appeared to be tons of cows. I hadn't gone ten paces when Michelle growled and leaped aggressively to my right side.

A split second of peripheral vision and I knew terror. Absolute, unmitigated terror.

Twenty feet away was a huge bull, a monster exuding crude, raw natural power. Repeatedly pawing the ground with his right leg, he stared at us, head lowered. He was pissed! Either that or anxious to show off for the legions of females crowding the fence. Whatever—we were the objects of his attention.

Michelle jumped toward him, barking. If he made the cows look small, she looked like a Minipin. The bull's response was simple: he charged.

"Leave it!" I ran for my life. I still had ten strides to go before reaching the fence when I could feel the breath of that beast on the back of my head. I wasn't going to make it! I zigged right, dove down through two posts, and waited for the bull to crash through the fence and right onto me as I rolled on the ground. But the crash never came.

At the last moment, Michelle had lured him away. To my horror, she was still fighting him. I climbed up on the fence, screaming, "Leave it! Leave it!" Finally, she responded, circled the bull slowly, then walked toward the fence. Again I yelled at her to come. Begrudgingly, she did. When she got to me, she turned back to the bull and growled.

I was so happy she was safe, I dropped to my knees and hugged her. My heart was pounding in spite of the overwhelming sense of relief.

A relief that lasted all of three seconds. Again a flash in my peripheral vision. Only this time I heard a human voice as well. I scrambled to my feet. I hadn't understood the words, but the malice in the voice was palpable. The flash I had seen was a mangy collie mix running with the farmer.

Suddenly everything happened very fast. The farm dog charged and Michelle lunged. He backed off, only to charge again. The farmer shouted, inciting his dog. His words were vicious. I stared the guy in the face and it seemed like forever before I heard what he was actually saying. He was strange-looking—an albino. At six feet or so, we were about the same height, though he appeared to be about sixty years old. He may have been older than me, but he was in great shape, which I could see as he was barechested under his farmer overalls.

But it was his head that was so unusual. He had the whitest hair and the ugliest, meanest face I've ever seen. His skin was light pink and as translucent as wax paper. Giant thumbs must have pinched his face together at the cheekbones to have created the visage I was staring at. His eyes were blood-red. Maybe they weren't, maybe that was my imagination, but that's how I remember it.

I certainly didn't imagine the shovel in his hands. He was poised to attack me, and off to my right Michelle was engaged in the first real dogfight of her life. We were cornered. We couldn't back off—the bull was right behind us.

The farmer advanced on us, shouting profanities. At the same time I could hear the terrible sound of clashing teeth mixed with snarls of anger and pain. I turned to help Michelle. Twenty years of dog training makes stopping a dogfight a reflex reaction. That's when I saw the farmer raise his shovel, coming at me.

I snapped into crisis mode: adrenaline pumping, no thought, just response. Maybe it was the sight of Michelle holding her own that fueled me, freed me up to go full bore against that farmer.

I hadn't been in a street fight since I was a kid in junior high but it all came back. I went for him. I was so scared, so pumped with fear, so sure that I was fighting for my life that I flew at him as fast and as hard as any cornered animal. Arm bent, my forearm and elbow took him square in the throat. A lucky shot. His knees buckled and he went down.

The momentum of my thrust brought me down right on top of him. It was the first time I had an opportunity to say anything. And with my forearm embedded in his throat, he had to listen.

"I don't want to fight, there's no need to fight. I'm on a search. A man is missing. The dog is a search dog. Please, I'm sorry. . . ."

That's what I was saying as I stood up. He responded by bringing his leg up to kick hard at my groin. His boot caught my thigh, thank goodness, but then he bolted to a half-sitting position and punched me in the face. I felt like I'd been smacked with the fat end of a baseball bat. I staggered back, only to plop into the mud, legs open in a seated position. I felt like I was in the middle of an awful nightmare, trying with all my strength to get somewhere and going nowhere.

I couldn't move, I couldn't breathe. I think I was on the verge of going into shock. All I could do was watch that farmer roll to his hands and knees and start to get up. Every second that passed felt like an entire day, and still I hadn't breathed. When I did, when my autonomic nervous system finally kicked in, I sounded like a deep-sea diver breaking the surface of the water. Heaving, I sucked huge amounts of air. The oxygen got me moving. And just in time.

He was already up and we made eye contact for one brief moment. His eyes were fiery red, filled with hate, and terrifying to me. He started to say something, then brought his arm up to his throat in obvious pain. On my knees still, I grabbed for the shovel on the ground between us and swung with all my might, slamming across his shins so hard his legs flew out behind him as the shovel flew out of my mud-slicked hands. He pitched face-forward into the mud. As he rolled onto his side, spitting and moaning, I staggered to my feet. Stumbling, I found the shovel again and headed for the dogs. Growling mixed with screams of pain and I couldn't tell which dog was hurt. Instinct kept me from calling out to Michelle, which was good. Listening to me now could get her killed.

I swung the shovel at the farm dog and grazed it on the rear end while shouting, "Get off her, you piece of dirt!" The dog yelped and let go. As it backed off, I said, "Leave it!" to Michelle and stepped between the two dogs, menacing the farm dog the whole time with the shovel. It backed up barking, but it backed up. That was the easy part: slipping into a position of authority with a dog is what a dog trainer does. The next step wouldn't be so easy: Michelle had to leave while saving face.

She was angry, buoyed by my presence, and ready to assert herself. She flew at the other dog with a snarl, broadsiding that cur so hard it fell and rolled over before it knew what hit it. Her speed and ferociousness stunned me. In all the years I had known Michelle, her gentleness and sensitivity, never had I seen this violent aggression.

She was on the farm dog before it could get up. Whacking the shovel on the ground near their heads, I was desperate to get them apart. Banging the shovel was as useless as trying to get the attention of sharks during a feeding frenzy. I was finally able to whack the farm dog on the butt once more, getting it to back up. When I said, "Leave it," this time, Michelle obeyed.

We headed for the woods in the straightest possible

line. Every few steps I turned to see if we were being followed. The dog stayed back. The farmer was still down, though he was sitting up. Quiet. As we entered the forest, I heard a single hollow bark but nothing more.

Hurrying us into the woods, I felt numb. As we walked, my body began to feel heavier and heavier, especially the left side of my face where he had punched me. Pretty soon I found myself walking with my hand under my jaw to keep my head up. Still breathing hard but with no sound of anyone pursuing us, I realized we had to stop and pull ourselves together.

I knelt to take a close look at Michelle. She seemed okay: no limp or stagger, nothing life-threatening. I could see several bloody wounds but I didn't want to stop moving. I had to get us as far from that maniac as possible. Checking my watch, I decided to plow ahead another twenty minutes or so, then we could stop. Again, we headed southeast. That meant a lazy turn to the right from where we had entered the woods. Good—that would make it more difficult for someone to follow us.

Twenty minutes later, I stopped, walked over to a tree, knelt down—and threw up. Rolling away, I leaned back against a tree, took some deep breaths and finally relaxed. Reaching for the canteen, I rinsed out my mouth. "Whew, that's the ticket." I was getting it together. Michelle, too. She was busy licking herself.

"Thank you, yoga," I said. "Meesh, come here, girl, and let me check you out." Michelle walked over very slowly, head swaying with every fourth step. She was limping slightly. I knew just how she felt. Now that the adrenaline rush was over, I could feel sore spots in my right knee and elbow, not to mention my swollen face.

"Let's look at you," I said. Her tail wagged slowly and she gave me a relaxed smile, a "it's a good time for a break" smile. I counted five bloody wounds including an ear torn at the tip. When she was a pup, the breeder had cut her ears much too short. Today, however, I was thankful for short ears—any longer and she might have had more serious injuries.

We stayed in that safe spot taking care of business for a good thirty minutes. The clearing was shaded by tall pine trees and offered us a soft bed of pine needles, just what the patients needed. Short of the heat, that is. I was drenched in sweat mixed with blood, some mine, some Michelle's. Of our two canteens of water, I used almost all of one for drinking and cleaning our wounds. Then I applied peroxide to Michelle's punctures and tears.

I have never known a dog as stoic as Michelle. In all our years of SAR work, I can count on one hand the number of times she's yelped in pain or fear. One of the few times happened near our house. I had heard her give out a loud yelp, then saw her come racing up from a stream bank with her head low and a guilty look on her face. Looking down the bank behind her, I saw a huge snapping turtle with claws that had to be three inches long! She's still curious about turtles, but gives them respect and a lot of space.

As we sat there on the pine needles recharging, I thought about that farmer. What had happened was so bizarre. Under normal circumstances, he would have seen us, invited me in and offered something cold to drink, drawn a map of the area and made a few phone calls to see if his neighbors had seen anything unusual. That's what usually happens when you meet up with local residents during a search.

Instead, he had treated me as if I was a dangerous trespasser. It was a reaction that made no sense. "I hope he's still licking his wounds and not after us with his gun," I said to Michelle. "Maybe he called the cops—I hope so." But even as I said that, I knew he wasn't the cop-calling type.

Ready to move again, we found the going much easier as we moved along deer trails under the shade of the pines. I darted from shade spot to shade spot, anxious to avoid any ray of direct sunlight. After a period of this crazy zigzagging, I stopped. What was I doing? What was wrong with me? Was I in shock? I realized I had been moving southeast in a spaced-out kind of way, my mind obsessed with the malevolent image of the farmer as feelings of fear and hate churned through me. I wasn't paying attention to the world around me.

Suddenly Michelle grazed my left leg, then disappeared. I was vaguely aware of having seen a dark shape, a shadow that vanished. Her touch was what I needed. It grounded me, brought me back to the reality of where we were and what we had to do. I never ignore a dog's touch, it always has meaning.

Grazing my leg was Michelle's way of communicating with me. She's worried, I thought. I'm not myself and she knows it, so she's checking in. It's as if she is asking me, What's up, what's happening?

I stopped abruptly. Michelle was gone. Then I felt her presence behind me and turned around. We were face-to-face. She gave me her bright-eyed "What's cookin'?" smile. I laughed, relieved, and squatted to nuzzle her. I am always amazed at the health benefits of nuzzling a dog; she gave me strength, strength to sit back and take stock again.

This time I was more focused. After all, I wasn't the victim, someone else was. I tried the radio again but still no contact. OK, I decided, we would continue the search but with a plan to be back to base camp by sundown. Michelle had not alerted to the victim's scent, I did not want to spend the night with mosquitoes, and, worst of all, I was not prepared for an overnight in the woods. I berated myself for my lack of preparation: You idiot, how many times have you told yourself that your search vest needs to be repacked and restocked for an overnight. Dammit! You don't even know what's in there.

"Michelle," I said, "here's the plan. I need to create a grid that will bring us back home. If we've been heading southeast, then we could go due west for a short distance, then northwest, then due east. We'll walk a parallelogram back to the road. That way we can cover a large search area, *and avoid that damn farm*. What do you think?"

Michelle wagged her tail slowly and cocked her head sideways as if to say, "I don't know, what do *you* think?"

We headed due west as I called, "This way, Michelle." Then I pointed in the new direction and said, "Go find." The two of us trotted off, renewed and excited. Michelle swung wide to the right, running parallel to my route. Confident of my direction, this allowed her to cover more ground. That is an understatement—if the wind is right, she can air scent a human being miles away. In comparison to what she can find as we move forward, I'm deaf and dumb.

As we moved on and she disappeared into the woods, I found myself feeling much better. She was enthusiastic and working. Even the wind was cooperating now with

a steady breeze from the west. Michelle worked into the
wind, which gave her some relief from the heat. Meanwhile, I had figured that I would walk due west for ten
minutes, then northwest. But that was the hard one to
figure out—how long would I need to walk northwest
in order to match the distance I had traveled earlier?
Getting back to my point of origin was critical.

The radio still wasn't working and it was now 1:30
P.M. We had been heading southeast for a good four and
a half hours. But how much time did we lose at the
farm? The sudden memory of the fight made the pain of
the injuries flare to the surface. I shuddered. It dawned
on me that my internal self had been uprooted by a storm
of such force that I was still suffering from mild shock.
About that time, I remembered the rough map I had been
given—no indication of any farm on that. Map, hell, that
thing was proving to be useless. I reached for the compass that should have been hanging around my neck and
was very relieved to find it still there. That's one ap-
pendage I cannot be without. No compass, I would be
as bad off as the victim in the car.

I was uncertain as to where we were and how far we
had to go. Fear was nagging at the back of my mind,
the awful thought of spending the night alone in these
woods. "What the hell are you scared of?" I asked myself out loud. "It won't be the first night you've spent
in the woods." But as I talked to myself and the trees,
sweat had begun to pour off me again.

I had a sudden out-of-body experience: I saw myself
from a distance standing alone in the woods and having
a conversation with a tree. The tree answered with a
shimmer of its leaves under the broiling sun: "It may

seem lovely but there is no comfort here; the mountains can be brutal, indifferent. Take heed."

I did, realizing it was time for another break, take some time to get myself together again, time to repair my inner self. I was feeling lost and afraid and I had to counter that. I sat down on a log to take stock. First, I'm thinking negative because of the farm from hell, I thought. Recognizing that made me feel better. I resolved to change my attitude; after all, backtracking this way we were sure to avoid the farm.

"I can do this," I said to myself. "No need to panic, I've done it before." At this point I really was talking to myself, repeating the very words I had said during a speech to the Rockland Kennel Club: "Panic, it's the number one reason for death and injury; it's what you hope the subject never does, it makes them unpredictable." The subject? How about the searcher?

Then I had a change of heart; the parallelogram walk seemed a poor idea. I decided to retrace my steps. I refused to consider that I might not be able to do that. After a few paces, I remembered Michelle. Hell, it would be nice if I told her that I had reversed direction. As I turned to call her, we nearly collided, I laughed as I said, "Doggone, you do know which way I'm going!" Her anticipation, her ability to know what I'm going to do before I do it no longer surprises me.

I used to think of myself as completely "flat" when it came to being psychic. The women in my family—Jaye, her mother, our daughters—they have an intuition, a "connectedness" that I've always envied. At times it has even frightened me. It would frighten you, too, if you lived with my family. Two experiences I'll never forget.

The first happened to Jaye's mother. She woke up one night in a sweat and heard a woman's voice say, "three more years." The voice was so compelling, Jaye's mom got up and wrote down the date. She tucked the slip of paper into a side compartment of her jewelry case and forgot about it. Three years later, her husband died of a heart attack. The day of his funeral, while looking for her earrings, Jaye's mom found that slip of paper—it was dated the day of her husband's death. Jaye was sixteen when she found her mother crying in front of the jewelry box with the slip of paper in her hand.

The other experience involved Michelle. It was early June and hot. I was home with Michelle and our other dog, Tri. Jaye and the kids were in school, teaching and being taught. I had a late-afternoon appointment that day, so I had finished lunch and was dozing in my EZ chair when Michelle woke me with her barking. More than that—she was standing beside me when she erupted into such a fury of barking that I was catapulted out of the chair in a state of near heart attack.

I tried to calm her at the same time that I thought my heart would go through my chest wall. She would have nothing to do with anything I said. Instead, she lunged for the door, hackles up, chest rigid, ears up, lips peeled back and a horrible growling in her throat. It was a "surround sound" experience combining malice, hate and violent aggression into something I had never heard from her before. The hair on the back of my neck went straight up.

"What is it? I don't see anything," I said as I approached Michelle. I knew something was up. As I always preach to my clients, dogs never bark for no reason. There's always a reason. It may be that *you* are unaware of what it is but the dog hears or smells something. That doesn't mean that you have to listen to the barking, which is why "quiet" is a great command to teach a dog.

But in this case, I didn't give that command. I had never heard such an ongoing, horrible snarl from Michelle. And the other thing was, she kept staring intensely at the door. Still, I looked out the window and could see nothing—nothing on the path to the garage, nothing down the drive to the road, nothing.

She kept it up, deaf to my initial "What is it, girl?" and deaf to my commands. I touched her in an effort to redirect her, but her body stiffened into what felt like a piece of immovable steel and the growling grew even more vicious. For the first time ever, she scared me. A sense of dread engulfed me as I watched, helpless to make any difference.

Then I saw him. A nondescript man of medium build, wearing khakis and a blue shirt, came walking down the road and turned left into my driveway. He walked up the drive to our brick walkway . . . and stopped. He could hear the dog barking from behind the front door. At a distance of about forty feet, he could make out me and Michelle behind that glass. We made eye contact but all I ever remembered of the guy was that his eyes were very black and they glittered. No detail of his face, just his eyes.

At that point, Michelle began to hurl herself at the glass door. I motioned to the stranger to stop and pointed to the dog. His body language in return was hesitant and angry and a shadow darkened his face as he looked at Michelle.

Then he did something very odd: he gave me the finger. After making the gesture, he turned and left. Michelle growled until he was out of sight.

Later that day, I told Jaye what had happened. She said that Michelle had been jumpy the night before, moving and checking the doors all night. Soon after, we heard on our local radio station that a convict, escaped from an upstate prison, was believed to be in our area. I called the sheriff and the description fit our visitor: khakis and a blue shirt.

I look back at that incident and I marvel. Under normal circumstances, Michelle would heed my commands of "quiet" and "stay," and I would respond to a stranger needing help. But this was different. She knew that guy was coming to our house well before he was visible, maybe before *he* knew he was coming here. We live on a quiet road but every day dozens of walkers and joggers pass by and Michelle does not go berserk. Alone, I may have let him into our home. But Michelle made it clear that she knew better. And I am forever grateful.

Retracing our path back went much easier than I had expected, so well that I started to feel good. Lighthearted, even. As I walked, I thought ahead of the friendly faces we would soon see: Frank, Ed, and, later, Jaye. Bouncing along with my daydreams, I suddenly realized I was off the trail and hadn't even noticed. Wherever I was, there was no sign of my earlier path.

"Major screwup," I said out loud. "You schmuck, all you had to do was double back on your own trail, all you had to do was pay attention. This was your big chance and now you're lost. This is *so* unprofessional!"

Everywhere I turned I saw heat spots. The afternoon air was so hot, my body was slick with sweat. My clothes were drenched and bugs were everywhere. The way I shunned the sun, anyone watching would have thought I was a vampire.

After a few minutes of searching for my original path, I gave up and checked with my compass. "I'll be okay," I assured myself. "I know the general direction, I can use the farm as a landmark and work back from there."

An hour later, I was so lost that I had begun to pray that I could find the farm. The farm from hell would be heaven, or at least familiar. Anything familiar would be a relief from the awful feeling in the pit of my stomach. Funny how quickly you can lose your confidence when you feel lost. I thought of the words I use with kids in my Hug-a-Tree programs: "Once you realize you're lost, don't keep trying to find your way back. Stay put. Searchers will be out there, wait for them in a clearing if you can."

Unfortunately, that did not apply here.

I read somewhere that true courage is being the only person in the world who knows you're scared to death. Well, lost and frightened is just not the image a K-9 SAR unit wants to portray. But this is not the first time for me, I must admit. In my early SAR days, I was so cocky that I referred to myself as "Mountain Man T." Then one Sunday in West Jersey, during a practice search, I got so lost the guys in my unit started calling me "Wrong Mountain T." And I had a working radio on that one! I had access to bearings and directions and I was still lost. Eventually, you find that you are not as lost as it seems and things do work out. I tried to re- member that right now.

I also tried the damn radio every few minutes, hoping for a miracle. In the midst of my struggle and worry, Michelle's cold, wet nose touched my hand. "You're not alone," she reminded me, and I felt better. Nudging my canteen and giving me a big smile, she indicated that she might be thirsty but *she* sure wasn't scared. My immediate reaction was to pour her some water at the same time that I thought we better conserve, too. "You should be finding your own ground water," I said as I poured.

Her demeanor, relaxed and happy, recharged me. I know that if I were to be very tense or worried, she wouldn't get scared. Instead, she would become protectively aggressive as she looked to shield me from whatever it was that threatened. Right now, it wasn't that bad.

"OK, time to regroup," I said. "We're on a mission to find a missing person but so far I have no indication— nor do you—that that person is within a hundred miles of here. Given that, our goal is to get back to our drop-off. If, on the way back, you tell me you smell another human being, we'll pursue it."

As I spoke, my real thoughts were more wistful: Gee, Michelle, I wish I had taught you to "take me back," then I could just give a command and follow you back to the road. I think she could read my mind because she gave me this quizzical look, head cocked to the side. "OK, OK," I said, "just remind me to teach you 'take me back' when we get home. Meanwhile, we'll use the compass."

Another hour heading northwest. Mentally and physically grueling. It was nearly three in the afternoon and I kept repressing the urge to find shade and rest until five or so. What kept me going was the reality that Jaye and the kids would be worried if I was missing, not to mention the humiliation of being the object of a massive search.

At this point, I figured Frank would assume my radio was down and have someone waiting for me at the drop-off. It was still too early for anyone to be too worried about my whereabouts. Nope, I would have to plod on until I reached civilization sometime.

I decided to head in a more westerly direction in case the road of my hopes curved away. I had made a mistake assuming that it went straight, but every time I examined the hand-drawn map, the road line stopped in the middle of the page. Another aphorism ballooned in my mind; "assume makes an ass out of u and me" took on real meaning. I had made so many mistakes, I felt stupid, like a rookie, like a screwup. And in fact, looking back, this was one of my early searches.

Water was now an issue. The dog is fine, at least in the Catskills where the mountains are lush with streams and ponds and swampy areas. Michelle was always able to smell water nearby, disappear briefly, and return with a dripping-wet face. Now, however, she was gently nudging for water from the canteen when I had less than half left. "Make do or go find some," I had to say.

I checked my supplies. I had two out-of-date iodine pills to purify water for myself in a pinch. I also checked nearby trees. Certain trees have vines, which, when cut can provide drinkable water. You have to be careful, though, that the liquid is clear, if it's cloudy or milky—don't drink it! Unlike dogs, humans cannot drink stream water—animal excrement can give you one hell of a case of the runs. Meanwhile, Michelle had executed two large sweeps and returned for more water—it was obvious there was none close by.

The forest was changing now, from new growth scrub pine to older deciduous trees, which offered more shade. The air seemed cooler, too. Again, I looked for a tree vine.

Just then Michelle took off at a brisk pace. Her enthusiasm tempted me to follow, which I did. She disappeared, and after a few minutes I was ready to call her when I heard her barking. It wasn't a working bark or a concerned bark, but a happy, playful, light bark. Following the sound, I entered a clearing with a large, gurgling stream and a little cabin! Civilization! Joy does not adequately describe how I felt as I watched Michelle swim and drink.

I didn't know what to do first, cool off in the stream or check out the cabin. I celebrated with a long drink from my canteen, then crossed the stream to the cabin. Before crossing, however, I took care not to get my feet wet. Soggy boots cause blisters and make a long walk miserable. As I moved forward, the idyllic scene took on all the characteristics of a mirage. The water proved to be brackish. And a look at the inside of the cabin put a quick end to my euphoria.

It appeared to be abandoned, though the doors were locked, which surprised me. The windows were caked with dirt and I could see scattered pieces of furniture surrounded by animal droppings. I did note a kitchen sink with faucets, but saw no sign of a telephone or electric lines into the place. As I was about to step off the decaying wood porch, a movement overhead caught my eye.

"Whoa!" I shouted as I stumbled off the step. I had looked right into the malevolent eyes of a huge wolf spider. He made it clear: this place is off limits.

"Michelle, let's go," I called. The house gave me the creeps and the spider didn't help. The field of spiders had been more than enough. I made an immediate mental note to avoid that field if we came upon it again.

The next few hours dragged on and on and on. I was feeling very sorry for myself as I trudged—the heat, the fatigue, the soreness and pain of my injuries, and the insecurity of it all. What a miserable march of hope. Hope? Yeah, hope that I would come across a road before having to spend the night out here.

Then it struck me: If I'm miserable, how about the missing person? How does he feel having to spend the night in the woods, probably very ill prepared?

About that time Murphy's Law kicked in and my watch stopped. Twenty-two minutes after four. The sun was low and I debated whether or not I should use what daylight was left to set up a decent campsite. Or should we keep going and bed down at the last minute?

Michelle was so tired, she sprawled out to rest every time I stopped for anything. And even though traveling in the dark would be dangerous, I knew how worried Jaye would be if I didn't return. I decided to wait until dusk, then climb a tree in hopes of seeing a car or house light.

As the light faded, I looked for a tall, climbable tree, both to climb and to use as a cover for a campsite. By now I needed a flashlight in order to read my compass and, sure enough, like everything else that had worked so well that day, the batteries were weak. I had another set in my vest but I was darned if I could remember if they were used or fresh. Again, I made a vow. This time it was to *be sure* to always have fresh batteries in reserve.

It was nearly dark when I found the right tree. I plopped myself down, saying, "Well, Michelle, it's just you and me." She pawed the ground as if to say, "Feed me" in response. At home she swats her aluminum bowl across the floor when she wants food or water. The bowl clangs across the floor and we all refer to it as Michelle's intercom system.

"You wait," I said, "first the tree climb because it's our last shot for getting home tonight. Besides, I don't think you'll be thrilled with this evening's repast." I couldn't remember what energy food I had grabbed before Frank had picked us up so many hours ago, but neither one of us was going to be very happy.

The tree was easy to climb. Halfway up, my heart left my chest when I spotted headlights. I hurried to take a compass reading of the mid-spot from where I first saw the car to where it disappeared, nearly falling out of the tree as I did so. It was tough to judge the distance, but it didn't appear to be more than a half mile. We got going. And going. It was taking so long, I worried that I had missed the road somehow.

Suddenly I stepped into the muddy water of a drainage ditch. With the sun down, the air was cooling and the ditch water felt icy, but neither Michelle nor I minded, we had a road!

The road ran east-west. I started west with no intention of stopping until we found another human being. We hadn't gone five minutes when headlights illuminated the pavement ahead. Even as I waved, the car pulled over.

"You Shelby?" said the driver. I nodded. "Get in, there's a lot of people looking for you." I walked around the old Jeep and directed Michelle into the backseat. The rear storage area was packed with junk. It felt like heaven to pull off my SAR vest.

"Sorry about the mud," I said.

The driver turned a strong, friendly face to me, "I'm Bill, a volunteer with the fire department. Are you OK?"

"I'm fine," I lied.

Bill reached for his radio, "This is twenty-two. I got a code green on Shelby, over."

Static, then Ed's voice: "Great, I'll call his wife. Is he OK?"

"Doesn't look like he's ready for the prom but he's in one piece."

Remembering why I was there, I asked Bill, "Did they ever find the missing driver?"

"No."

I leaned back into the seat and took a deep, relaxing breath. The tension drained away. Leaning against the open window, I looked up at the sky. Someone had scattered diamonds across the heavens.

Aftermath:

The driver of the car with the blood on the windshield called his insurance company the next morning to report that he had swerved to avoid a deer and hit a tree. Because it was nearby, he walked to his girlfriend's house. Later I heard that she had picked him up in her car, which explains why the dogs never picked up his scent.

Michelle's injuries were superficial with the exception of a deep gash on her underbelly.

Jaye told me I was a hero—her hero anyway. She treated me like a king for the next two days.

Training Notes

Training and the Shock Collar

Countless times I've been asked the following questions: "What are your training methods? Do you use food? A choke collar? Shock collar?"

What people really want to know is how I train a dog. While their approaches to me may vary, mine to the dog is always the same: "Depends." I am like a psychiatrist who may see classic similarities between patients, yet recognizes that each is different and requires a personal touch. And so it is that I'm a "depends" trainer treating each of my subjects as a different character.

How do I train a dog? Timing, body language, voice intonation and perseverance are mixed with gentle firmness. I use what will be the most humane, effective and quickest method—in that order. That may include shock collars, which usually elicits a look of dismay.

Because the shock collar gets that response, I would like to show you how and when it is right to use it. I got a call about Olivia, a black lab, three years old, who was copraphagic—eating poop. Her owner was beside herself. "Olivia is perfectly trained, goes everywhere with me off-leash, listens to everything I say, I couldn't ask for a better dog but—"

"But what?" I said.

"Well . . . when I take her to the dog run in the park for exercise every day, the moment she gets there she covers the area like a mine sweeper scooping up all the turds. I can't stand it anymore."

She wasn't exaggerating. I walked with Olivia and her owner down to the aforementioned park. She was as responsive and cooperative as Lassie—but as soon as she entered that dog run, down went her head, she started quartering at high speed with her nose two inches above the ground, and sucking up turds every few seconds.

I knew instantly that the "most humane, effective and quickest" solution was . . . the shock collar. I also knew that I wasn't the first trainer called in on the problem. Another guy had chased Olivia around throwing cans at her and shouting "Leave it" until he slipped and fell in the poop himself. The image made me grin.

"I think we can fix this pretty easily," I said, after watching Olivia perform.

Several days later we were back at the run, but this time Olivia was wearing a shock collar set to give a mild shock. As she dashed into the run, I had my hand on the remote control. The second her head dropped for the first tasty morsel, I hit the button. Olivia felt the discomfort of the mild shock just as she picked up the first turd. She immediately dropped it and hopped to the side as if touching the turd was the cause of the shock. Perfect timing!

She waited then reached for it again. Once again she was made to associate the picking up of fecal matter with a shock and hopped back.

"What's going on?" asked the owner, astonished.

"I shocked her twice," I said, without taking my eyes off the dog for an instant, "and she'll probably need one more today, a couple tomorrow, maybe one the next day and that should be it." Sure enough, a few moments later Olivia's head dropped for another try. I made sure it was in her mouth before she got zapped. We stayed another fifteen minutes but there were no more attempts at snacking.

As far as Olivia was concerned, I did nothing but praise her in the dog run; it was the turds that gave her a hard time. And so I turned the remote over to her owner with a list of dos and don'ts and told her to call in a few days with results.

She called the next day to report Olivia had spent an hour at the run and needed the shock only once. The next call came three days later to thank me. No more zaps had been needed. I congratulated the owner and instructed her to carry the remote, while keeping a sharp eye on Olivia, for three more weeks. If there were no more incidents, she could leave it home.

For Olivia, the shock collar was humane, effective and quick.

6
Cakewalk Search

*So there we sat, my editor, Susan, and myself, dis-*cussing my final draft of this book. I thought I had completed the writing, I thought I had said everything there was to say about Michelle and me. Susan thought otherwise.

"How come there are no perfect endings, Tom?" she said. "You know, like 'Michelle saves the day, finds the missing child alive and they all return happily ever after'?"

"What about the search we do in the chapter titled 'The Blizzard and the Unsung Hero'?" I countered. "I consider Michelle responsible for the live find of that kid."

"Yes, yes," Susan continued, "but I'm talking about a rescue where Michelle runs up to a crying kid and the tears turn to smiles as she barks happily at his side while there's a heartwarming reunion with the parents. You have nothing close to that in the whole book."

I looked at Susan and said in a deadpan voice, "In that blizzard search, the kid's mother fainted dead away with relief when I radioed in that her son was found and OK. I wasn't there, but I heard that she was unconscious before she hit the floor, hit it hard."

"Not exactly what I had in mind," my editor retorted.

"Well, let me tell you some realities about live finds, Susan," I said. "An SAR trainer like myself can easily train and search with three generations of the greatest search dogs in the world without experiencing a live find. That translates to twenty years of working a highly trained and motivated dog, twenty years of searches and never finding a live victim. Why? Because there is a very real element of luck involved—the proverbial being in the right place at the right time. . . ."

SAR is voluntary, an adjunct to my life's routines. Discounting practice searches and training, if I go on six or eight actual searches in a year, that's a lot. When I get to a search site with my dog, several basic factors must be in place if there is to be even a possibility of a live find.

First, there has to be a missing person. Ask any searcher about false alarms and you'll get the same list: the person who is not lost but somewhere other than where family and friends expect, the person who is just fine but hasn't called home in a while, the one who is drunk, or the one who appears to be missing but in fact there was some simple miscommunication over the time or place of meetings.

Second, let's assume I'm at a search site and someone is actually missing. For there to be the possibility of the live find, the victim must still be alive. I've been told that, statistically, most finds are deceased.

Third—and this is the big one—the lost person has to be in the area where I'm searching! This is a big world. As you know from my earlier search stories, I always try to start a search at the location where the missing person was *last seen*. What does that really mean? Often nothing.

The person missing for twelve hours or three days can be anywhere. Unbeknownst to anyone I may have spoken to, the missing person could have hopped a plane and be in Portugal. Or a man could be really lost but sixty miles away from where we're looking because he decided to hunt in a different area at the last moment, but didn't take the time to inform anyone.

But let's say he is in the general area where we're searching and we have four search dogs to cover a fifteen-square-mile area. Each K-9 team will get a grid, a portion of that area to search. If the victim happens to be in your grid, in that microscopic area of the wide world that you're searching, with a good dog and a little luck you have a live find.

For Michelle and me, a live find happened on our very first call-out for the Rockland Sheriff's Department. And, as it turned out, it was this search that led Jim Kralik, the sheriff of Rockland County, to talk me into going through the police academy and becoming a cop.

I got the call around ten at night in the late fall. It was Kralik himself calling to ask if I would bring Michelle and help search for a seventy-four-year-old man who should have returned from his walk before dark.

"Where are we talking about, Jim?" I asked.

"Kakiak State Park," he said. "The man's wife called

us at about nine. We found his car in the parking lot. I've already sent in a couple of mounted units, but I think you and Michelle have the best chance of finding him the quickest. His wife told me that he was wearing shorts and a T-shirt and had no flashlight. And it's cold out now."

"Is the command center at the victim's car?"

"Yes."

"Good," I said, "I'll be able to scent Michelle off the car seat. We'll be there in about twenty minutes, but please do me one favor, Jim—please make sure I can get inside the car. Until we get there, seal off the area to everyone. Make sure no one goes near the inside of that car, especially the driver's side."

"Consider it done. Good luck and thank you," he said, and that was the last I heard from him that night.

Quickly I called Larry Frenkel, one of my closest friends. I called him for a couple of reasons: he lives next to the park and knows his way around the area as well as anyone because he hikes it all the time. Matter of fact, we've hiked it together many times. Most of the hikes we took were at night, often under a full moon. After those hikes we liked to go back to his house and sit in his hot tub with fat cigars while watching the clouds flirt with the moon.

I also called because I wanted him as my co-op. I knew that the Sheriff's Department would have at least one deputy accompany me because this was police business. Such searches require a police presence in the event there may be a suicide or foul play. But my co-op on a search is my personal partner and assistant, and although I've used cops and firemen whom I just met as co-ops in the past, the idea of sharing something like this with Larry appealed to me because of his knowledge of the park and his familiarity with Michelle and me. He's also one of my closest friends and right up there when it comes to people I can trust under any circumstances.

As it was, his wife, Ronda, answered my call, then said, "Larry, pick up, Tom says he has an adventure for you."

He got on the phone and said without even a question, "Let's do it—I'm up for a walk."

"It's more than a walk," I said. "This is a search for a seventy-four-year-old man missing in Kakiak."

"You serious?" I could hear the excitement in his voice.

"Meet me in Kakiak's parking lot in a half hour. If you get there before me tell the cops that you're with me. Be prepared for an all-nighter, Larry—fresh batteries and extra water."

Jaye was already putting together energy snacks for Michelle and me while shooting questions. She had heard my conversations with the sheriff and Larry and knew a little of who and where, but she wanted details, details that I didn't have.

"Who is it that's missing?" she demanded. "What do you know about him? Do you think he's really missing? How long have they been searching already? How many people are out there looking? Do you think the woods are already contaminated by searchers?"

The bustling about the house had Michelle's attention because it was not the normal routine she observed most nights. And when she saw my SAR vest come out, she instantly clicked into full alert mode. Her eyes never left me and every once in a while she would give out a short whine of excitement and impatience. She knew what was coming.

The moment I got into my truck for the fifteen-minute ride to Kakiak State Park, I felt edgy. Something was nagging at me, something wasn't quite right. I reviewed all my preparations to be sure I hadn't forgotten something important. Then it hit me—the snakes!

Kakiak County and state parks have the largest rattle-snake dens in New York State, and a park ranger once told me that poachers come from all around the world to pilfer rattlers from this region. Two poisonous snakes are indigenous to the area: timber rattlers and copper-heads, and Kakiak is rife with both, not to mention many varieties of nonpoisonous snakes. I've seen snakes on many of my daytime hikes through that park, but only once have I seen one at night. Unfortunately, it was a copperhead.

My greatest worry is for Michelle. She has never had snake-aversion training and would be likely to check out any snake she found just out of curiosity. Now, if I'm there and looking at her, I can yell, "Leave it," and she'll back off. But in the dark of the night the odds of my being able to do that are miniscule. Not only is she off-leash, but all I can see of her most of the time is the glow necklace around her neck. Boy, did I wish I had taken the time to get hold of a snake and give her snake-aversion training.

I then did the next best thing. I called my vet at home and asked him to please make sure that, in the event I needed it, I could get antidotes for both copperheads and timber rattlers. He said he knew that the Oradell Animal Hospital had both on hand.

As I pulled into the parking lot and saw all the flashing lights, I was reminded of the flashing lights that I had seen in this very same spot just two nights earlier. The memory brought a smile to my face.

Larry and I had decided to take one of our night walks into the Kakiak and I had stupidly parked on the dirt road entrance to the fire lane. After our walk, right around 11 P.M., we were approaching my car when Michelle started barking. Suddenly, we were blinded by flashing lights and a huge spotlight trained right on us. It was an officer from the Sheriff's Department. They patrol the state parks, which are officially closed after dusk. Add to that the fact that I was illegally parked.

The irony was that I had just been deputized by the sheriff to assist when a K-9 unit was needed, so after an apology on my part and my display of my Special Deputy ID, Larry and I were back on our way to his hot tub.

"Well, now you see that cock-and-bull story I told one of your guys two nights ago about the dog and me being a search unit turns out to be true," I found myself saying within a few minutes.

Meanwhile, the parking lot held the usual small crowd of police and ambulance crew. I told Michelle to wait in the truck while I was filled in on the details. Then I assessed what I wanted to do. We were ready to go, but state and local jurisdictional squabbling delayed our start for a good forty minutes. Finally, I complained, "There's a seventy-four-year-old guy out there who's definitely not getting any warmer waiting for us to find him!"

At last one of the officers came over to where Larry, Bill, Michelle and I were waiting by my truck. "We opened the car with a slim jim," he said. His name was Bill, and he was assigned to accompany us on the search.

The rest went very fast. I brought Michelle over to

the missing person's car, turned to Larry and Bill, and said, "Be ready to move out. The moment Michelle scents the car seat, she may take off." I pointed to the car seat, and on my command "Go find," she jumped up, put both her paws on the seat and snorted it. Then, without hesitation, she turned directly around and, nose to the ground, headed for the closest trail entrance at a brisk pace. I had to tell her to wait in order to slow her down a few times. But the search was on.

We crossed a large footbridge spanning a wide stream and soon came to a three-way fork that required no decision because Michelle took the path farthest to the right without hesitation. And so it went for half an hour. Michelle walked with deliberation and we followed her rights and lefts.

Only once did I say to Larry, "You know where we are now?"

He stopped, looked around and said, "No problem."

Then we both laughed.

"What's the joke?" said Bill. But before we had a chance to answer, he figured it out. "Never mind," he said, "it's obvious." Looking at me, he said, "I bet you've heard 'no problem' from your pal here on more than a few occasions, but with less than perfect results. Am I right?" Now we all laughed.

"The man's got the making of a detective," Larry interjected.

"We grow and learn from our misadventures as well as our adventures," I said with a grin.

After another few minutes, I noticed that the pace was picking up. It was harder to keep Michelle in a range that allowed me to read her, to see if there were any changes in her intensity.

"Wait!" I called out. I was catching only glimpses of her green glow necklace. She was still going down the middle of the trail, but she was moving faster, and, best of all, I was seeing the telltale sign of darting. While I couldn't see Michelle's body, the glow ring's movement was jerky, a sure indication that she was "hot"—jumping from scent pool to scent pool.

This is when my heart always starts beating against my chest. It's the moment before the climax of a search. Once the missing person is found everything that follows is anticlimactic. The search is at its most intense when the dog's body is humming, that's when you know you're about to find a missing person!

Michelle was working excitedly, her nose had gone to the ground; she wasn't air scenting, she was tracking. The night was brisk and clear and the trail we were on was about five feet wide with the trees forming walls on both sides. Michelle was about a hundred feet ahead of us and moving fast, heading for what looked like a clearing but turned out to be a power line cut in the woods.

What happened next happened so fast that it surprised me. Before I could share with Larry and Bill that Michelle had just announced an imminent find, she came to a stop in the middle of the clearing and growled. As I got close, I could see her hackles up, but I couldn't see why until the beam of my flashlight fell upon the figure of a man. The moment I saw the shorts and T-shirt, I knew it was our victim. *We had a live find.*

"Hi," said the guy sheepishly.

"Are you Peter Connors?" I asked.

"Yes, I am, sorry to put you to all this trouble," he replied.

Michelle was still growling softly. Up to that point, every live person she had ever found had been found during a practice search and the found people always responded with great zest and praise for Michelle. This person's subdued response made her suspicious.

Meanwhile, Bill and I were already on either side of Peter, each of us giving an arm for support as he looked a little shaky. We sat him down, and then I called Michelle over. I praised and kissed her as though I was elated, which was easy because I *was* elated.

Then I went into our routine that I use to celebrate her success: I grabbed a stick and threw it for her to retrieve, then I continued to praise her for what a great stick she had. After she retrieved the stick we had a short tug-of-war, I let her win, and she pranced away, head high. She was filled with pride and joy as I congratulated her on her wonderfulness.

"I took a shortcut and got lost, then I ran out of daylight," said Peter to Bill and me. Then he turned to Larry and apologized again for the trouble he caused us.

"No problem at all," said Larry. "We walk here all the time. As a matter of fact, Tom and I took a three-hour hike in here two nights ago, we do this for fun."

"Well, thanks all the same," Peter insisted.

The walk back was slow, steady and uneventful. I noticed that Peter had taken his long wool socks off his feet and put them on his hands, running them up his arms for extra warmth. After he declined medical help, he was driven home—delivered safe and sound.

Larry, Michelle and I took the five-minute drive to Larry's hot tub, where we luxuriated with fat cigars, celebrating Michelle's first live find of a missing person.

This having been Larry's one-and-only K-9 search-and-rescue experience, he announced while we were both submerged up to our chins, "You know, T, this search stuff is a piece of cake, a real cakewalk."